UNPLANNED DESTINATION

UNPLANNED DESTINATION

ELIE JEROME

Library of Congress Control Number: 2017910033

Elie Jerome, Brooklyn, New York

ISBN: Hardcover   978-0-9965510-3-8

ISBN: Softcover   978-0-9965510-4-5

ISBN: eBook   978-0-9965510-5-2

This is a work of fiction. The events and characters portrayed are imaginary. Their resemblance, if any, to real-life counterparts is entirely coincidental.

This book is dedicated to Miriame Rose Louis and all those who have perished during that devastating earthquake on January 12, 2010. Sorely missed, but never forgotten.

ACKNOWLEDGEMENT

I am speechless and more than thankful to the Almighty God who grants me life, health, knowledge and a creative mind to write stories. All the glory to you.

I thank my family and friends who supported me throughout the whole writing process.

I will be forever grateful to all the wonderful readers and supporters of my first novel, I Dare You To Try It. You guys motivated me by asking me non-stop, "Elie, when is your next book coming out?" Your excitement built my confidence in writing. Thank you.

Profound thanks to my line editor, G. Miki Hayden. She amazed me with the way she communicated.

Before I even pressed the send button, she already replied to me.

I had the privilege to work with amazing editors, Karen Bowman, Vicki Thompson, Josephine Farella, Georgiann Bothwell, and Mikelson Blemont. Thank you so much for your time and dedication. A tip of hat for all staff of Division of Cardiology in Maimonides Medical Center, they welcomed all my questions and surveys. They never got tired of me. They supported more unconditionally.

In addition, I wish to express my sincere thankfulness to all my Facebook friends, Judith St Surin, Fatton S. Francis, Jackson Francis, Pedro Charles, Angelo Marcelin, Reginald Fils-aimé, and many others who provided me great insights to make this book a good read.

A special thanks to Mark Reid, my book cover designer from authorpackages.com.

And from the bottom of my heart, I thank all of you who bought the book.

Earthquake

January 12, 2010, Port-au-Prince, Haiti

Around four p.m., I headed to the main road and caught a bus. A few minutes after I took a seat, an abrupt and strong vibration jerked me out of my imaginings and brought me back to reality. *What kind of concrete drill are they using to build the road?* I asked myself. The bus stopped in the intersection of Lalue and Avenue Christophe.

All the passengers, including me, glanced at each other in confusion with the hope that one of us could explain the strong shaking of the ground. Seconds later, we heard a loud scream, dust surrounded us, and we couldn't see further than two feet ahead. Everyone including the driver got off the bus and ran.

The dust became thicker and limited my vision to the point of my nose. Since I was aware of the tense and hostile political climate within the country, I thought maybe someone had blasted a bomb near the National Palace. I didn't panic, but I was afraid that I had taken the wrong direction and might bump right into the chaos. I tried to run and ran into two people. "What's going on?" I asked the second person.

"Earthquake, earthquake," he said in a distressed voice before disappearing into the dust. *Earthquake?* The first and last quake I'd experienced was in August 2005, when I was at the house of one of my ex-girlfriends, Sherley. During that tremor in August 2005, Sherley clung to me, and I laughed. I found the tremor beneath my feet amusing. From that experience I could never have pictured an earthquake as a hazard capable of causing such strong damage to human lives and properties.

When the dust became thinner and my vision cleared, I glanced around me and muttered, "Holy God!" All the houses on the entire block where I stood had collapsed. I freaked out, and my knees trembled. I saw a female student crawling out from a collapsed building—her school.

"Help me, help me," she begged.

I stood frozen in front of her as my brain tried to recollect the definition of the word *Help*. I found myself with a dilemma. Should I run like everybody else to find my family, or should I rescue that student? Once I regained my composure, I leaned toward her and tried to help her stand.

"I can't. My…my… my…other leg….. Other leg is under the wall," she stammered.

I looked at the wall and I would definitely need a superpower to remove her leg from under it, or I would need to hammer the wall down. *Where would I find that hammer?* I panicked. I'd trained at the Haitian Red Cross, but nothing about rescuing people was mentioned during those classes. Now, I spotted a huge piece of round steel; I slid it under the wall. I pulled, I pulled, I pulled with all my guts and soul, yet the wall didn't budge an inch. The ground shook one more time. I sprinted into the street.

"Repent, repent, it's the end of time," a man shouted as he was running.

I looked the student in her eyes one last time, shook my head, and ran toward home. *Will you let her die, Leito?* my heart asked me each step of the path while I edged away from the student in distress. Half a block further on, I made a U-turn and came back to help. I grabbed the piece of steel and lifted it as much as I could, but still with no result. A few seconds later, two other hands grabbed the steel, and we lifted the wall off of her leg.

"Thanks," I said to the man who'd helped me save the student. The man and I carried the student away from the building. The man looked as though he had plunged his body in a bag of beige sand. No need for a mirror, the man's face gave me an idea of how my own face looked at that moment.

Like ants, people were screaming and running in all directions. On my way home, I saw that the National Palace and many other federal buildings had collapsed, including the National Penitentiary, which had allowed many convicts to escape. In no time, I was already in Martissant 15, where I spotted a gas station on fire in Martissant 19. Less than fifteen seconds later, a propane tank from the gas station bounced everywhere and headed in my direction. People screamed. "Let's go into that alley," someone shouted.

I quickly entered the alley and ran. I saw people standing and watching as the tank continued on its path. Along the way, people said the same things to their friends and family members, "Thank God, you're still alive. Did you see X and Y? What about Z?" Some answers were positive and others negative. Everyone wanted to go home and check on their family.

I continued my marathon and along my journey witnessed people covered with dust, bleeding and screaming for help. Dead bodies lay all over the sidewalks. Cars were parked pointing in all directions. Finally, I reached home. My entire family was safe and sound. We hugged each other like never before and said, "Thank you, Jesus."

But that was neither when my story began, nor when it ended.

Here with a Message

July 24, 2007

On a Tuesday afternoon in the summer of 2007 in Martissant, one of the slums in Haiti, Anita, a widow and mother of two sons, was washing clothes in front of her hovel when two male strangers stopped in front of her. Both men appeared to be in their early twenties, about the same height each—five feet, six inches tall. One wore a green hoodie, dirty worn Levi blue jeans, and a pair of black and white Adidas EQT 1998. The other man had on a black polyester jacket, dark-blue cargo pants, and a pair of Tommy Hilfiger white flag sneakers that looked beige from all the dust.

"Is Ronald here?" the stranger wearing the green hoodie asked.

"Where's your manners? Who raised you?" Anita snapped. "No greeting... Is Ronald here? Like I owe you."

"Nobody has time for this," the visitor said. "We're here with a message. Is anyone else here?"

"No. Only me," Anita replied.

"We want to give a message to your son, Ronald."

"No problem. I'll make sure he receives it."

The man wearing the black jacket pulled out a Glock 17 from underneath his jacket and took aim at Anita.

Anita's eyes widened. "Jesus, save me," she shouted before he racked the slide on his gun and emptied the entire magazine into her.

At the sound of the gunfire, people screamed. Those close to the shooting jumped over walls, ran into other neighbors' houses, or ducked—any way they could take cover and stay alive.

The shooter then took out a fresh magazine from his cargo pants pocket and stuck it into the handle of his handgun after removing the emptied one. "Let's go," he said to his companion, who also pulled out a Smith & Wesson Model 10 from underneath his green hoodie.

People remained in their havens with their hearts beating almost out of their chests as more gunfire reverberated. The two gunmen left behind a horrible scene in the neighborhood. In the aftermath, a total of thirteen people, ten men including two boys, one eleven years old and one of fourteen years—plus three women—joined the afterlife.

A few minutes later, Claude, Ronald's brother, came back from school and found his mother dead on the floor next to a washbowl full of clothes. He was enrolled in a free mechanics program at a public trade school. Holding his notebook in his bare hands since he couldn't afford a bag, Claude stared at the colander-like body of his dead mother, mangled from all the shots in her chest. Sunk in trauma, he couldn't say a word.

"Drink this," one of the neighbors said, and he handed a spoonful of olive oil with salt to Claude. The neighbor stood next to the boy and looked at Anita on the ground in front of her unfinished, one-room house built by her husband. The house wasn't completed because they couldn't afford a mason.

A piece of plywood served as the doorway for Anita's house. The crooked walls of the house represented a mystery for many in the neighborhood. At first sight, anyone would bet that a human being's breath could dismantle the house. Yet, the home remained standing after resisting more than twenty years of strong winds from hurricanes.

"C'est la vie, (that's life)" the neighbor said before he sighed and patted Claude's shoulder.

Anita, also known as Tata, a wonderful, down-to-earth, respected, and peaceful woman of fifty-four years old, was a symbol of hard work and the dedication of Haitian women to their family. For over thirty years, Tata had traveled miles and miles along the roads selling oranges to get the money to educate her sons. She carried about one-hundred pounds of oranges on her head every single day. Even though she had never sat in a classroom in her entire life, she believed education would bring a better tomorrow to her children.

"What pain… What pain," a mother cried out as she saw her only son dead in front of her house with a science book in his hands. That boy of eleven years old had been studying when he heard the gunfire. Instead of seeking safety, he'd walked outside to see the face of the gunmen, and his curiosity had cost him his life.

While the inconsolable mother screamed even louder at the feeling of gut-wrenching grief, a neighbor took a dress and wrapped it tightly around the woman's belly. When people were facing horrible pain, Haitians believed a piece of clothing well tied around their waists would help them bear the pain and prevent the soul from fleeing the body.

The neighborhood turned into a makeshift morgue. The carnage brought everyone out in anguish. Many tried to guess a logical reason behind the bloodbath.

The secret didn't take much time to be unraveled. A throbbing voice crying for vengeance echoed into the neighborhood, followed by two gunshots in the air. Ronald, the older son, had received the devastating message. Right after he pulled out the gun, many neighbors became aware of Ronald's involvement in some illicit activities.

Two rival gangs, Bone for Bone and The Iron Teeth from two slums in Martissant, a southern district of Port-au-Prince, were at war. They were shooting and killing each other almost every day. Ronald had joined Bone for Bone a few months previously.

A few weeks before, during the opening day of a soccer tournament, Ronald alone killed five members of The Iron Teeth, including three soccer players, for his initiation into his gang. Ronald thought his action would have brought fear to his enemies; instead, he'd doomed his entire community. Neighbors, close friends, and family members weren't spared the wrath of The Iron Teeth.

Ronald was bulky with braided hair and dark-brown skin. His body looked like a painted canvas due to all the tattoos he had. A huge tattoo of a lion breathing fire on his left arm grabbed people's attention right away. Many said he could have been mute because he never used more than ten words to express himself. Due to illness or simply natural to him, he was born with red sclera, which granted him the nickname of Bloody Eyes.

Three days after his mother's wake, while Claude stood in front of a deli with a friend, a gunman fired at them. Claude jumped in a ditch next to the deli where people disposed of all their trash. With cuts on his face, and smelling like a dirty portable toilet, Claude climbed the gully a few minutes later, hoping that his friend, too, had survived.

Unfortunately, Claude's friend didn't have the same kind of luck. He lay face against the ground, a bullet in his head, and with flies starting to land on his bloody cheek. The neighbors, in tears, held their heads with their hands and asked when this violent storm would come to an end.

Such attacks reoccurred. The members of The Iron Teeth told Ronald that death would be the only way out for him and his brother. The Iron Teeth, a small armed gang created in 2004 for political reasons, had grown in numbers and equipment over the years. Like a virus, they terrified the entire city and slipped out of the control of their own creator.

Ronald knew he wouldn't be able to protect his little brother. He feared the worst—his only brother being murdered without trying to protect himself. Ronald loved his little brother and best friend very much. He handed a Beretta 92FS to Claude and then said, "Kill or be killed."

Against his will, Claude abandoned his dream of becoming a mechanic. He joined his brother in the gang Bone for Bone to avenge his mother's murder and protect Ronald, his only remaining family member.

Claude had been great at school, polite and discreet—the opposite of his brother. He had a slim body, was clean cut and had no tattoos. His neighbors praised his kindness when comparing him to his brother. During his childhood and teen years, he was barely involved in any kind of trouble.

The rivalry of those two gangs escalated to a level that even the Haitian police couldn't control. Many people fled those neighborhoods. Before seven a.m. and after six p.m., any man from another area who found himself walking in one of those two gang members' territories was either harassed, mugged, or simply killed. As the conflict continued, more people died with greater casualties on the Bone for Bone side.

Houses built right next to houses, no road access in those slums, and lack of intel made handling that conflict an impossible task for an underpaid and unequipped police department. The cops took a step back and watched the two gangs kill each other. The cops felt there were no innocent victims here. The victims were all accomplices, either by implication or by not sharing information with the police.

"We can't sit and watch our family and friends die every day like this," a neighbor said following another attack led by The Iron Teeth. "We need to cut Bloody Eyes into pieces with machetes. If not, he'll get us all killed." That neighbor became angry after losing his best friend, Wilfrid, a well-known merchant of charcoal within the neighborhood.

"His sidekicks as well," another neighbor shouted, referring to Ronald's brother and friends.

Two days later, following a rainy night, Claude assassinated the two neighbors who'd tried to conspire against his brother. Many thought Ronald had killed the two, which increased their fear of him.

One early afternoon the entire Bone for Bone, the remaining eighteen gang members, were having lunch inside an abandoned house. Some standing, others sitting on a bench, they were eating and laughing when a man wearing burgundy oxford shoes, black pants, a white shirt, and a grey jacket walked in and stood in the doorway with his hands dipped into his pocket.

"I'm here to talk," the stranger said before he took off his sunglasses.

"Who said we wanna talk?" Sony, the headman of Bone for Bone, asked as he pulled out a Ruger Single Six. "Don't you see we're having lunch?"

"You should ask yourself, do you wanna eat one day or eat every day," the stranger replied.

"I'm listening," Sony said once he realized the sight of his revolver had no effect on the stranger.

"I'm a captain and I'm here with my right and left arms." The visitor pointed out the windows where two other men stood—one with a Mossberg 935 and the other one with an AK-47. Both men aimed at the gang members inside. "We're cops. We want you to work for us."

The gang members glanced at each other in panic, but a few managed to look calm. Some thought about reaching for their guns, and others wanted to sprint into the back of the house. Then they all realized it was too late.

"Guys, relax," the captain said.

"How can we be relaxed with guns pointing at us?" Sony asked.

"For safety."

The captain explained his plan to the Bone for Bone members. He told them that he would provide guns and ammunition to fight against The Iron Teeth if they worked for him. He also promised they would make a lot of money.

"We're not interested—fuck the cops!" Sony replied before he spit on the ground.

"Okay," the captain said as he put his sunglasses back on and turned to walk out of the room. His two wingmen already had the order—leave no one alive in case of a negative answer.

While the captain was about to take his last step to exit the room, he heard someone choking and something fell on the ground. When he turned his head he saw Sony coughing up blood with a knife stuck into his neck—by Bloody Eyes, eager to avenge his mother's death by any means necessary.

"I'm in charge now," Ronald said to the captain after he pulled the knife from Sony's neck and wiped the blood onto the palm of his left hand.

The captain looked at Ronald, nodded, and then said, "Good, at least one of you has a working brain."

"Can't stand cowards," Ronald added.

The other gang members hadn't expected such an act from Ronald, but none of them felt sorry for Sony. They admired Ronald for his bravery and fear of nothing.

"So you want us to do your job?" Claude asked, stepping forward.

"Kind of..." the captain replied.

"Since when have the police started recruiting," Claude asked.

"As of today."

"What's next?" Claude asked.

"You keep doing your thing on the streets, but I'll tell you where and who to hit," the captain said. "Before any cop makes a move on you, I'll let you know."

Ronald remained silent while his little brother negotiated with the captain. However, he didn't take his eyes off the other two cops standing by the window.

"And then?" Claude continued.

"We split the ransom in half," the captain replied.

"What if we keep everything we take?"

"Sure, if you want the entire police department after you guys. I hope you know that you're on the most wanted list. After all, finding you wasn't hard."

"Understood," Claude said. "But what guarantee do we have that you'll keep your word?"

"That's the same question I ask myself about you," the captain replied.

The captain's shiny oxford shoes made the Bone for Bone members wonder if he came from outer space, or was the man so bad that even dust didn't want to mess with his shoes. The captain's appearance gave a glimpse of his fine taste and class. Making eye contact with Ronald and Claude, the captain projected the image of honesty.

Claude glanced at each man of the gang for their approval. They all nodded as a sign of agreement with the contract, which sounded risky, but fair.

"I need a gun for shooting at a distance," Claude said.

"Do you know how to use one?" one of the captain's wingmen asked.

Claude turned his head and glared at the captain's wingman.

"He asks, so he knows," Ronald replied with a bit of aggressiveness in his tone.

"Say no more. I got you," the captain quickly said to calm the tension. "Give me your number, and I'll call you in two days. Pick up any private caller ID."

Two days later, the captain provided many handguns and shotguns to Bone for Bone members and a Remington Model 700 to Claude. Even though he had a dark heart filled with envy and greed, the captain seemed to be a man of his word.

In less than two months, Claude alone killed sixteen Iron Teeth members. He managed to kill only the members of the gang and left behind almost no collateral damage.

Indeed, Haiti was considered the poorest country in the Western Hemisphere economically, but it was full of unlimited natural and human resources. Claude was a living legend who could have been one of the best snipers the world has ever known. The US had Chris Kyle; Haiti could have proudly told great tales about Claude —if the country had had an army. At soccer, basketball, and even with bouncy balls, he was the best and one of the most gifted men.

Many stated that Claude sold his soul to the devil in exchange for his ability at killing people. In Haiti, most of the citizens didn't believe in talents and efforts. Whenever someone achieved greatness, people linked it to either corruption or voodoo.

While Ronald kept pursuing his tactic of bringing fear with his bloody and wild acts, Claude turned his neighbors into his shields. To redeem his brother, Claude gave money to the people, especially those who'd lost their loved ones, to open their own businesses. He also promised to keep them safe from The Iron Teeth. In return, the people became his eyes and ears in the streets, spying and extracting important information.

Knowing about the presence of any visitor in the neighborhood took Claude less than five minutes. He wanted to build an empire. In his neighborhood, they called him *Father with a good heart*. To some people, Claude and Ronald represented an imminent threat to society; to others, they were simply two necessary evils.

As time went by, the captain provided more guns and ammunition to his recruits, and Claude and Ronald became the most notorious criminals in the capital of Haiti. They gained an outstanding reputation for kidnapping, drugs, and assassinations, the majority of which were ordered by the captain. Money, drugs, guns, and ammunition—they had it all. Many other youths joined the gang. The name Bone for Bone soon belonged to the past; the gang name changed to the Gillette Brothers.

In Haiti, people used a brand name to identify an item even from a different brand. All refrigerators were called Frigidaire. All shaving blades were Gillette, and all cereals were corn flakes. They referred to Ronald and Claude as the Gillette Brothers for their sharpness and quickness at doing damage to others.

Trust Me

"License and registration, sir," the cop said in a firm tone.

The driver had failed to stop at the red light and almost hit a pedestrian. At around one-thirty p.m., the streets were congested with business people and students leaving school. Trash that hadn't been picked up was strewn all over the road, which worsened the traffic.

"How are you, chief? It's hot as hell, and you're doing a hell of a job," the driver replied with a smile on his face before he reached into the dashboard of his car to take out his registration. The driver appeared to be in his early twenties and wore a black suit with a sky-blue shirt.

The cop felt flattered that at least one citizen had acknowledged his efforts in that one-hundred-and-five degree weather. He responded in a more polite manner, "What can we do? Somebody has to do the job," before he wiped his forehead with his bare hand.

After receiving the requested document, the cop looked at it and then asked, "Where's your driver license?"

The driver smiled at him and confessed, "Chief, I'm not gonna lie to you. I'm a mechanic, and I have a date with a beautiful young woman who I think will be my wife. It's our first date, and I wanna make a good impression. So, I took one of my customers' cars."

The cop shook his head in disbelief, smiled at the young driver, then said, "She will take you for a boss, and you don't even have a driver's license. On top of it, you don't respect the traffic regulations."

"Chief, you would have done the same if you had seen that beautiful woman. Trust me."

The cop couldn't deny the driver's comment. As a gentleman, he knew a good impression counted on a first date because it set the tone for any future relationship. They chatted for a few minutes. The cop even gave the driver some tips for going out on a first date.

"When you see her, get out of the car, kiss her on her forehead, and praise her beauty. Show her that you're affectionate," the cop said.

"I'm going straight for the lips, chief," the driver replied.

"You don't wanna mess up her makeup, do you?"

"You're right. Didn't think about that."

"Open the car door for her. Ask her questions about her night, her family, how she feels, and so on. You need to show her that you care about her," the cop continued.

"Right."

"Wherever you're taking her, let her choose. Women love to feel that they're the number one priority."

"That's true," the driver replied.

"If you see a homeless person nearby, give him some money. She needs to know that you're a giving person."

"Thanks a lot, chief."

The driver paid attention to the cop's advice. However, he kept going back and forth in his seat behind the wheel.

"What's wrong with you and that seat?" the cop asked. "Are you stressed?"

"If you were in my shoes, wouldn't you be?" the driver replied.

"Why?"

"I still don't know if you're gonna give me a ticket or arrest me for driving without a driver's license."

"How can I give you a ticket if you don't have a driver's license?" the cop said before he walked around the vehicle, a grey Mitsubishi Montero Limited 2004 with plate number TZB 40562. "I like your attitude and I won't mess up your date. Here's a ticket just in case another cop stops you." The cop handed the registration back to the driver.

In Haiti, when someone committed a traffic violation, the cop used to confiscate the driver's license and give the person a ticket. The driver would pay the fee and retrieve the license at the motor vehicle department. It then became a practice for people who didn't have driver's licenses to find cops they were friends with to get a ticket for the violation. In case any other cop stopped them, they wouldn't get arrested.

As the cop made his way toward his police car, the driver stepped out of his vehicle. He called the cop, gave him a handshake, and said, "Next time, I will make my driver's license bigger."

The cop was vexed when he looked in his hand and saw a five-hundred Gourdes bill that was less than fifteen US dollars. "What the f…! Turn around with your hands behind your back."

The driver had mistaken kindness for corruption. His saying the driver's license would be bigger meant that he would give more money the next time. A few corrupt cops used to stop drivers and collect bribes. Those cops stated that the police department didn't pay them enough money to make ends meet. That practice by a few officers had tarnished the reputation of the entire police department, with the trust by the population already low.

The driver realized he had made a big mistake. He obeyed the cop and hoped he could convince him to not arrest him. The driver said in a low, calm voice, "Please forgive me. It wasn't my intention to offend you. I just wanted to thank you for being so kind to me."

The cop pushed the driver against the SUV before he handcuffed him and brought him to the police car. He put the driver in the backseat then jumped in behind the wheel. The officer looked at the handcuffed driver and said, "You fucking pissed me off. I should have whipped your ass."

"I know, and trust me I've learned my lesson. Please save my date."

In his rearview mirror, the cop watched the driver apologizing for his guilt. He felt that he should forgive him because the driver looked like a very polite citizen. As the cop was about to let the driver go, he heard the following message on his walkie-talkie from the police department: "There's a crime in progress. One man got shot in front of a bank in Delmas 35. The suspect is wearing a black suit with a sky-blue shirt, driving a grey Mitsubishi Montero Limited with plate number TZB 40562. The suspect is about five feet, nine inches tall, dark skin, and black hair."

The cop took the young driver to the nearest police station—his assigned precinct. As soon as they stepped into the police station, Marc, the commander there, shouted, "Claude Gillette." He looked at the cop and continued, "We've been looking for this guy day and night." Marc welcomed Claude with two slaps on the face. Marc slapped Claude so hard, in fact, that Claude fell over onto a table.

Another cop, by the name of Paul, walked in. He pulled a Colt M1911 from his auto-lock holster then hit Claude three times with the back of his pistol. "Stand up, jackass."

As Claude managed to stand up, blood started pouring from his head.

"Throw that jackass in a cell," Marc commanded some officers.

All the officers in that police station came to witness the arrest of one of the most ruthless criminals in the country. They cheered at the big catch. They couldn't believe that Jean-Baptiste, a rookie cop with ten months of service on the force, had arrested Claude by himself.

"That was a big catch. Go home—you're done for the day," Marc commanded Jean-Baptiste.

As satisfied and proud as he was, Jean-Baptiste couldn't believe he'd caught Claude. The outdated picture of Claude at the police station and the way Claude was dressed and talked would have tricked any cop. No one expected to see an outlaw wearing a suit in a third world country. Jean-Baptiste got carried away with his thoughts and felt that they should award him rookie cop of the year.

The news about the capture of Claude by a rookie cop spread among the police stations within the city. Patrick, the police commissioner, called Jean-Baptiste to congratulate him. Patrick also advised Jean-Baptiste to be more cautious and call for back-up next time. Claude was the most lethal criminal the country had ever known.

As Jean-Baptiste started driving home, he recalled the back and forth that Claude was doing with the seat. He made a U-turn and raced to the place where he'd stopped Claude. He arrived just in time to prevent a tow car escorted by two cops from removing the Mitsubishi. Jean-Baptiste opened the driver's side of the car, looked under the seat, and found two fully loaded Beretta 92FS. At that moment, he understood exactly what the police commissioner meant by telling him to call for back-up next time. The other officers searched the vehicle and found a number of other guns and ammunition in the SUV, enough to equip a quarter of the cops at a Haitian police station.

Jean-Baptiste got back into his car—trembling in fear. He realized he had come very close to death. With a pounding heart, a lead foot on the pedal, and a shaking body, he drove home to his family.

The next day, the police transferred Claude to the main Haitian prison called the National Penitentiary. Many considered the National Penitentiary a nightmare spot. Ten men could be jammed into a small unsanitary cell with three beds to share, not to mention the length of time a person not yet convicted had to wait before seeing a judge.

The citizens found great satisfaction and relief at the news of Claude being captured. Some people said the police should have killed him for what he did to innocent people, which would have served as a warning for other criminals.

That accomplishment, among many others by the Haitian police, showed improvement in the honesty of the officers and helped them gain trust within the population. The majority of the cops now thought it was just a matter of time before they caught Claude's brother, Ronald. Ronald became the number one priority for the police department. They increased their patrols within the capital. Yet they couldn't chase him within the slum even with the help of the United Nations soldiers—the MINUSTAH, which had been established in Haiti in June 2004 and were still present.

The Usual

All Mighty was the name of the barbershop where Marc, the commander-in-chief of the Delmas police station who'd slapped Claude, went to have his hair cut. The shop usually had two barbers, but on this day one of them had called in sick, due to a fever. With a relatively small space of about one-hundred square feet, the barbershop had two hydrolic barber chairs, two mirrors on the opposite side of each chair, one bench for waiting customers, one AM-FM radio, and some posters of haircuts and soccer players attached to the walls.

"I'm surprised to see no line today," said Marc after entering the shop.

"They're coming later," the barber replied before dusting hair from the chair and inviting his customer to take a seat.

Activity at the barbershop looked slow on that early Friday afternoon. Customers would sometimes wait hours to get their hair cut; some even scheduled their appointments in advance because the barbers were quick and talented. After four haircuts, the customer would receive a ten percent discount on the fifth cut.

"The usual," Marc said to the barber before he sat down.

As Marc was getting his hair cut, he started listening to a young man about twenty-five years old named Fredson talking about politics.

"Every time I come here, I see you. Why don't you look for a job?" Marc said to Fredson.

"Chief, without a godfather or a godmother, I can't get a job. You know better than me," Fredson replied.

"It's who you know rather than what you know," the barber added.

"But I believe God will open a door for me," Fredson said.

"Do you have a resume?" Marc asked.

"I don't."

"Even if you had one, what would you put on it ?" the barber mocked.

"What do you mean?" Fredson asked the barber.

"Come on, man, be honest with yourself," the barber replied.

"What can you do?" Marc asked Fredson.

"Many things, chief. I finished high school seven years ago."

Marc shook his head in disbelief. In Haiti, many wanted to travel, work, and have a job. Meanwhile, they had no passport, no resume, no diploma nor skills. They went to church every day, hoping that God would make a miracle for them.

"Why don't you learn how to cut hair? You could make some money while you're waiting for your godsend," Marc said.

"I'm thinking about it."

"Hmm... Don't listen to him. He's lazy. I tell him that every day. If he'd taken my advice, he would have been a barber these last three years," the barber said.

"So you're looking for a desk job ?" Marc asked.

"All of them want to be doctors, lawyers, accountants, but none wants to learn trade professions," the barber said as he referred to the lack of interest of the Haitian youth to learn a trade.

"You know work gives you freedom, right?" Marc said.

"I know, chief, but I don't bother much because I'm also waiting for my residence visa. I think I'll go to the US soon," Fredson said as he stretched his legs.

"I've heard about you traveling soon for years. Every day, it's the same song," the barber stated as he reclined Marc's head to shave his beard.

"The USA is not paradise. You would have to work your butt off. Rain or snow, cold or hot, you have to clock in and clock out. Life ain't easy my friend," Marc said.

"Have a seat. I'll be with you shortly, fam," the barber told the man who'd walked into the barber shop and appeared to be a customer.

Since the man remained standing, the barber turned his head toward the man to ask him to sit. Right after the barber turned his head, he panicked.

"Are you okay?" Marc asked when he felt the barber's hand shaking next to his chin. Since he received no answer and heard nothing from Fredson, Marc glanced at the door and saw a man standing in front of it with a gun in his hands.

"Marc, you know who I am?" the man said.

"Yes, you are Ronald Gillette," Marc replied with a shaky voice at the surprise of Ronald knowing his name.

Fredson and the barber glanced at each other. They heard on the news the damages caused by Ronald. They thought about escaping, but there was only one door to exit—and Ronald stood in front of it.

"*Bat chen an tann mèt li*, (Hit the dog and wait to meet his master)," Ronald said. That Haitian proverb—Hit the dog and wait to meet his master—meant if one does something bad to someone, that person who has done the bad deed will face the consequences of the act from someone else. Ronald now fired three shots into Marc's head. The barber and Fredson stood there speechless.

After killing Marc, Ronald pointed his automatic Colt 45 at the barber's head.

"Oh! Oh! He was just a customer. He wasn't my friend. I didn't know him," the barber pleaded, his hands raised in the air as he urinated on himself while trembling in fear.

"You shouldn't be cutting his hair," Ronald said before he pulled the trigger twice—leaving two bullets in the barber's chest. The barber fell on the ground face down.

Ronald turned his gaze on Fredson, who realized his life had now come to an end. He shook his head and shouted, "Oh, Lord, you let me die without seeing the US," before he gasped.

"*C'est la vie*," Ronald said. Pow. Ronald shot Fredson in the chest. The bullet landed straight inside the victim's heart.

Right before he left the barber shop, Ronald called the captain. "Give me the name of the fucking cop who arrested Claude."

"Jean-Baptiste Fleurimont," the captain said and then hung up the phone.

The people who came to witness the bloodbath in the barbershop, walked out in tears with their hands over their mouths or their faces cupped in their hands. Many ascribed Marc's murder to an act of vengeance. Three weeks before, Marc had gone to a party and slapped a man who was speaking with his fiancé. In his town, Marc had built his reputation as an honest cop as well as being a very jealous man who often overused his power.

As the Haitian economy collapsed, factory jobs and attending the police academy became the most sought after ways to access jobs. A police force insufficient to serve the fast-growing population, kept losing its members under the wind of insecurity that blew any day, any time—like a tree losing its leaves during the fall season. No wonder the statistics showed a ratio of one man for seven women in Haiti.

The police arrived at the bloody scene and put together a report on that incident. They assured the families of the victims that they would find the criminal and bring him to justice. After collecting the information needed, they left the barbershop.

A neighbor said, "More victims added to the list of 'the investigation is ongoing.'" This sentence was used by many to say that justice remained an illusion within the country.

That Friday morning, Fredson's aunt whom he lived with had a dream and warned him not to go to the barbershop. Fredson chose to be stubborn and go. In an ironic twist, that same afternoon, Fredson's aunt had brought a letter inside from the USCIS, inviting the young man to come to the US embassy for an interview in preparation to receive his green card. The timing of that letter mystified an entire family already in despair, especially Fredson's parents who lived in Fort Lauderdale.

Are You Good at It?

One of our neighbors passed away. He died after having a heart attack. He'd been a mentor to the youth who grew up in Thor 67, a neighborhood in Carrefour City. Everyone gathered to support the family and close friends.

Since early 2000, many things had changed in Haiti. Back in the day, the family of the deceased gave coffee and tea to the guests who came to sympathize, tell jokes, and play cards and dominoes. Such visits after a death used to be a moment when people were reminded of how precious life was and the importance of cherishing every single moment spent with their loved ones. That routine no longer existed in people's mind. Guests didn't expect coffee and tea. They wanted beer, liquor, and food. What used to be a moment of meditation had turned into a celebration. However, the family here made some cinnamon tea with ginger just in case someone requested it.

Three weeks before, a beautiful woman named Miriam along with her mother rented a house in the neighborhood. Every man started chasing her. I had heard of her presence from my cousin Junior. Miriam was single with no kids and mistress to a married man. In that short period, people had already extracted a great deal of key information about her. Junior told me many men were looking for an opportunity to start a conversation with her. But most of the time, Miriam was either with her boyfriend or sitting in front of the house with her mother. The wake represented a perfect opportunity for those men to court her.

As soon as I walked outside, I saw Miriam sitting on a chair surrounded by men as though she were presiding over a conference. She wore a grey miniskirt with a black sleeveless t-shirt and flip-flops. With her provocative body, Miriam became the main attraction of the wake—all eyes were on her.

I greeted every man with a handshake. When my eyes met Miriam's, I said, "Good evening, neighbor."

"Good evening, neighbor. Are you always late to everything?" she asked.

I looked at her and smiled. Miriam had caught me off guard. I didn't expect her comment.

"I was studying. That's why I came late."

"Okay, no problem."

I kept moving. I walked inside the house of the deceased and greeted the other people. I should have stayed a bit with Miriam to continue the conversation, but I didn't want to show her too much interest. I used the economic theory of supply and demand. The more offers she got, the higher the bid would be. Also, I didn't have to rush anything since she'd signed a one-year lease. Her house was about forty yards away from mine.

Junior followed me inside and whispered in my ear, "Why didn't you continue the chat with her?"

"Relax, player," I replied.

"Don't disappoint me."

"I got this," I said before he opened the door and walked back outside.

I wore navy-blue cargo shorts with a white V-neck t-shirt and black Nike sneakers. I then sat down on a chair for quite a few minutes to meditate about my new neighbor. An undeniable beauty, Miriam symbolized the power of creation, a shining diamond, and the most powerful magnet in human history. Such a shining light kept all men awake. Even Stevie Wonder or Andrea Bocelli would have glanced at her and described her beauty. At that moment, I understood why she had become the holy grail of the neighborhood.

Jean-Baptiste and his daughter came inside to sympathize with the family. They greeted everyone and then took a seat next to me. A few minutes later, Junior came back inside and said, "Yo man, why don't you come outside? You're not interested?"

"Chill, player," I said to him with a wave of my hands.

"S.O.S., one day somebody will whoop your ass and Junior's over his woman. Watch," Jean-Baptiste said to me and Junior.

Junior shook his head and walked back outside. I could see the feeling of disappointment on his face, but I couldn't reveal my master plan. I had arrived late because I knew she was outside and a lot of men were already at her heels. Dessert is served at the end.

Jean-Baptiste called me S.O.S. after his wife had related to him two dreams she'd had. In the first dream his wife was in the middle of the sea and drowning. Jean-Baptiste stood too far away to rescue her. So I did. In the other dream, she saw Jean-Baptiste walking on a mountain. He tripped on a big rock, and then slid toward an abyss. Jean-Baptiste tried to hold on to everything around him as he went down, but in vain. That abyss looked so deep that he had no way to make it out alive. When he was at the very edge, I came from nowhere, grabbed him, and saved his life. Jean-Baptiste made fun of me and bullied me whenever he could. As a prideful man, he found it odd that another man would save not only him, but his entire family.

When I moved to Thor 67, Carrefour City in 2001, my relationship with Jean-Baptiste started in rivalry. We played for two opposing soccer teams in the neighborhood. Since neither of the teams could pass the semifinals, they merged in 2004. Jean-Baptiste was very much against the idea. He stated that I was too slow in the middle field. The first year, he never played with me—either he or I would be on the field. So, I barely played since he was the face of the team.

In 2005, one of the players, Mikelson, moved to New York, which opened up a spot for me. Yes, I was slow, but my ability to create space for my teammates became paramount. They called me "Boss" because I made everyone score, and when I passed the ball they said it was a check. I was blessed to play with some amazing soccer players: Venel, Edwidge, Mario, Hugede, and Jean-Baptiste. They made it so easy for me. On the pitch, Jean-Baptiste and I developed a good chemistry that turned into a great friendship off the field. That same year, we won the tournament and had won twice in the past four years.

Very athletic with the physique of a body builder and the strength of a bulldozer, Jean-Baptiste had earned the name "the Animal." About two-hundred-and-twenty pounds, five-foot-eleven, mahogany complexioned with frizzy black hair and an oblong face, Jean-Baptiste was handsome and devoted to his wife and two kids. Besides his extreme jealousy and his inability to control his emotions, Jean-Baptiste was a skilled martial artist and the best friend someone could ever have in life.

"What a waste! We made the tea and nobody wants to drink it," one of the family members complained.

I stood up, grabbed a pot with a few cups, and volunteered to serve the tea. I started offering the tea, and many rejected me.

"Why don't you shower yourself with the tea? It can lower your blood pressure," one of the neighbors mocked.

I chuckled and continued to offer tea to those who wanted it. As I reached Miriam and her admirers, she said, "How come you served everyone before me?"

"I was coming to you," I replied with a guilty smile.

"What if there was no more tea?"

"I would have made more for you."

"Next time, remember, ladies first," she said. "I thought you were a gentleman."

I smiled and gave her a cup before I poured the liquid into it.

"That tea is good. It's hot and sweet," she said after the first sip. "I like it, neighbor!"

"Do you want some bread?" I asked.

In Haiti, coffee or sweet tea is always served with bread.

"No thank you," Miriam replied.

I smiled and continued to serve the others. After Miriam accepted the tea, every man wanted to drink tea including those who'd rejected it at first. So many people asked for the tea that the family ended up making another pot.

Once I finished giving out the tea, I joined some neighbors who were playing dominoes at a table with four players competing against each other under one rule—every man for himself. The one who finished with the most points would carry a concrete block of about twenty pounds on his shoulder until someone else took the spot—fourth place. The player with the second highest points, third place, yielded his spot to anyone else who was waiting to play. That rule made the dominoes game fun, and more people got a chance to play.

Before my turn came, I watched one guy named Pétion bragging about being the best player at the table. Pétion stated that he had been playing for hours. He never left the table nor carried the twenty-pound concrete block. Great or lucky, no one could argue with his statement.

On my second time of playing at the table, Pétion came in fourth, while I was third. He had to wait for me to play before he did. I made it very difficult for him and made fun of him holding the concrete block for a couple of minutes. As time went by, Pétion started to complain about the weight of the concrete. Every time Pétion adjusted the concrete on his shoulder, I said, "If you don't quit, your shoulder will have to be amputated." The others kept laughing, and Pétion got angrier. His eyes turned red as though he was ready to shed tears. The fun of playing and challenging Pétion took my thoughts away from Miriam until Jean-Baptiste called me over.

"Are you crazy?" Jean-Baptiste whispered after grabbing my left arm to pull me aside.

"What are you talking about?"

"Do you know who Pétion is?" Jean-Baptiste asked.

"Why should I know? We're just playing dominoes," I replied naively.

"This man is the devil in the flesh, well-known for his secret and terrible magic weapon called *yesterday I saw you.*"

Yesterday I saw you was a magic powder used by people with an evil intention to kill others. That evil powder would take someone's life away in less than twenty-four hours. Only a true Christian or a voodoo priest with high power could bring that person back to life, and the likelihood of finding one of these was at a very low percentage.

I had no idea that I was playing with fire. That vital news got my heart racing at more than a hundred miles per hour. As a precautionary measure, I didn't return to the table to play dominoes. Instead, I joined the crowd that surrounded Miriam. I sat down on the corner of a bench next to a neighbor named Maurice with my mind going crazy about what Pétion thought of me or could have done to me.

As I regained my composure and started listening to the conversation of my neighbors and Miriam, I realized all the men were doing the same thing—trying to impress her. Some bragged about their sexual endurance. Some talked about their possessions. Others told jokes to catch her humorous side. Many men had already been rejected while others lurked around waiting for their turn to start a conversation with Miriam and to ask for her phone number.

"Neighbor, you're sitting in the corner and aren't saying a word," Miriam said to me.

"I'm listening."

"Cat got your tongue?" she joked.

"Leito, my cup is empty," Maurice said.

I looked at him and said in my mind, *Does he take me for his servant or his bartender?* I smiled, stood up, and went to refill the big pot I'd used to serve the tea. Maurice tried to mock me; I acted as though I didn't understand.

While Miriam was lighting her entourage with her smile, a huge shadow of hatred and jealousy started to spread. Many women glanced at her in dislike. They gathered inside the house to gossip about Miriam, not because they knew anything about her, but she represented a threat to their relationships. They created all types of negative stories about the new neighbor. I heard one of them say, "Look at that cunt! She'll give AIDS to all those dogs at her heels."

Open-minded, Miriam listened to all comments and had a nice way of turning any man down. We lived in a small country with people of a narrow mindset. Miriam was one of the rare women who broke the barrier of the idea that the man should approach the woman. Haiti faced many such rigid customs at all levels on top of all crises that blocked its ascension on the road to development. They labeled as a whore or gold digger any woman who socialized with men for short periods of time.

Miriam had obviously become tired of her admirers, but being polite, she pretended to be entertained. They had no substance in their dialogue. I wondered if those men had any clue how to court a woman.

"What were you studying, neighbor?" Miriam asked me.

"I'm getting ready to take my CPA exam."

"Really, you're an accountant?"

"Yes, ma'am."

"Those men who change nine into six, six into zero," Maurice mocked.

"Are you good at it?" Miriam continued and paid no mind to Maurice's comment.

"It's like second nature to me."

"I'm struggling with Accounting 1, and my professor doesn't explain the concepts very well. Many of us find it quite difficult," Miriam said.

"It's not that hard."

"Would you mind helping me with my accounting class in your spare time?"

"I'll be more than happy to do so," I replied.

Miriam seemed very interested in accounting. This subject had turned into a mental escape route for her. She asked me all types of questions about the subject. Since many of the other guys knew pretty much nothing about accounting, they left the space one after the other. In about thirty minutes, only Miriam, Maurice, Junior, and I remained on the porch.

Tired of the accounting subject, Maurice said to Miriam, "Can you call my phone for me? It didn't ring all day. I don't know if..."

Miriam didn't let him finish the sentence; she said, "Give me your number."

Maurice told her his phone number. She dialed it, and his phone rang. He looked at the screen of his phone and then shook his head. Her phone call came up as a private caller ID. Maurice wanted to have Miriam's phone number. She'd surprised him with that unexpected move. He thought he was slick, but she'd outsmarted him.

Maurice, a gas station owner, believed everyone had a price, and money could open any door. In a poor country like Haiti, he couldn't go wrong. Even though he helped many people financially, his arrogance was obvious to all. Knowing Miriam had a married man as boyfriend, Maurice felt he could place a price tag on her.

Finally, Miriam and I changed the subject to bring everyone back into the conversation A few minutes later, I saw Miriam looking at her phone. Before she even said anything, I stood up and said, "It's bedtime for me."

"Oh, you came late, and you're the one leaving before everybody else," Miriam said.

"He has to go to bed so he can study tomorrow morning," Maurice added.

"Come on, man, stay with us for a little bit," Junior said.

"Next time. Good night, folks."

I waved at everyone and walked toward my house. I didn't have any plan. I was just playing with Miriam's mind. Maurice apparently felt great satisfaction at my departure.

Less than twenty minutes later, Junior came home and told me that Miriam had also gone home. He also expressed his disappointment regarding my behavior that night. He thought I should have been more aggressive toward her. Junior also confessed that he needed me to build a bridge for him because Miriam had a niece named Judith whom he liked very much. Junior said he was confident that I would succeed if I chased Miriam, and he would then get together with Judith as well. We spent a good hour talking about our plan to conquer Miriam and Judith.

Junior and I formed the best team ever. We had great chemistry like Jordan and Pippen. Whenever we walked into a house, I brought attention to me, which gave Junior a space in which to operate. By the time they discovered him and switched their attention to him, I'd scored.

Bad Intention

On a Monday, around three-fifteen p.m., the sun was hidden by some clouds and leaves falling from the trees following a soft breeze. Santa Maria High School had just released its students. Parents and children stood on the sidewalks, waving their hands for public transportation in both directions. The excitement of the young people after their first day of school created a commotion in front of the building.

Traffic was usually heavy from two-thirty p.m. to six-thirty p.m. in Bourdon, the road that led to Pétion-ville, a city considered to be the Manhattan of Haiti. What should have been a one-way street turned into a two-way street, and the main road for mass transportation. Added to that were drivers who stopped in the middle of the road to drop off and pick up passengers.

A young cop about five feet, nine inches tall, in his late twenties, ducked behind a wall and watched a young woman with her daughter leaving the school area to catch a bus and go home. The woman and her daughter were holding hands and smiling at each other when the young cop came from behind and covered the little girl's eyes. He shushed the mother to not say a word and left the little girl wondering who had covered her eyes.

The mother laughed and then asked her daughter, "Guess who it is, Johanne."

Johanne, the little girl, kept smiling and mentioned the name of two classmates. Wanting to help Johanne, her mother gave her some hints. "It's a man."

Johanne couldn't guess who that man could possibly be, but for sure she had a feeling that he was someone very close to her. Some male teachers' names came into her mind. However, she doubted any of her teachers would dare to play such a game with her.

"Please, Mom, tell me who is he," she said in a gentle and innocent voice.

Her mother kept laughing and didn't give her the answer. Once the young cop uncovered her eyes, Johanne turned around and shouted, "Daddy," before she jumped in his arms.

On Johanne's first day back to school and her birthday as well, her father wanted to surprise her and wish her happy birthday. He had to work overnight and wouldn't be able to be with her for the rest of the day. The young cop held on tightly to his precious treasure—his only child. He kissed her on both cheeks and surprised her with a gift.

Johanne wanted to open her gift and unfold the secret hidden in that nicely wrapped box, but her mother told her to wait until she reached home. Johanne knew the wait wouldn't be long and decided to enjoy the affection she was receiving during those few minutes before her father had to go back to his duties.

The mother admired the love her husband showed their only child. She felt proud and satisfied.

The young cop was teamed up with another officer named Paul, the one who'd hit Claude in the head with the back of his gun. They had to patrol the streets in a Toyota Land Cruiser for the rest of that day. Paul, a great guy with a lot of good moral values, got out of the Toyota and walked toward Johanne and her family. He greeted and congratulated the mother for having such a beautiful child before he wished happy birthday to Johanne with a kiss on her forehead.

"Daddy, can I have an ice cream please?"

"No, you'll be home soon," the mother said. "You have to eat first and then you'll get dessert."

"It's her birthday. Please let her have an ice cream, my treat," Paul said.

"No, no, no, we got it, Paul," replied the young cop.

"I know you got it, but I wanna be part of the birthday party," Paul said as he took out his wallet and gave the money to Johanne's mother.

"Okay, honey, what flavor you want?" the mother asked.

"Vanilla and chocolate," Johanne replied.

The mother walked across the street toward the ice cream vendor, and the two cops continued to chit-chat. Meanwhile, two men on a motorcycle were coming in their direction through the traffic. They pulled over a couple of feet away from the two cops.

Ronald, the man sitting on the back of the motorcycle, got off, walked toward the two cops, and fired at them with his automatic Colt 45. He shot Paul first with a bullet in the head. As the young cop was diving for cover, Ronald shot him three times in the back.

Normally, the young cop would have reached for his gun and fired back at Ronald, but his daughter in his arms was his Achilles heel. The life of his daughter became his priority. The young cop fell face down on the ground.

Despite his weakness, he managed to protect his daughter by not falling on her.

Total chaos took over, and everyone leapt for cover. People ran in all directions; passengers inside buses and cars ducked—scared of being hit by a flying bullet. The young cop found the strength to turn on his back in order to see the face of the man who'd shot him. As the young cop was coughing up blood, his daughter hugged him and yelled, "Please, Daddy, stand up! Stand up, Daddy." Poor little girl—her birthday was spoiled by a dreadful surprise.

Ronald walked closer to the young cop on the ground and pointed his gun at him. The young cop, out of breath, said, "I beg you to spare my life. I never did anything wrong to you."

"I have no mercy for cops," Ronald replied.

"It's my daughter's birthday. Please give me that chance, and God will bless you."

Johanne quickly took her father's gun, pointed it at the killer, and said, "If you touch my father, I will kill you."

Ronald looked at Johanne and said, "Bad intention, little girl."

Time stopped, and the door of hell opened up. A loud scream echoed from almost all the witnesses, reaching the deepest part of the firmament when the empty casing hit the ground right after Johanne fell—dead. Ronald had put a bullet in her head without any hesitation before he got on the bike with Ali, his henchman, and vanished in the streets.

At that moment, the young cop's eyes became red with the blood of vengeance. What a tragedy! An innocent thirteen-year-old girl killed in front of her school—on her birthday. Some students trembled in shock, while others screamed with fear and in disbelief of what they had just witnessed.

Lately, Haitian citizens seemed to have become cowards. More than seventy people witnessed the horrible scene and not even one of them tried to stop the criminals. "United we stand" had turned into "everyone for themselves." Like smoke in the air, pride, courage, morality, unity, and other key values disappeared from the souls of the daughters and sons of the brave Haitian ancestors who signed for the freedom of the nation with blood for ink and bayonets for pens.

Many people surrounded the young cop. Some held their heads with their hands while others speculated about the incident.

Johanne's mother stood by the ice cream vendor and stared at her murdered child and her husband dying on the ground. She felt an unbearable pain. Deep in shock, she kept saying, "Oh, oh, oh..." as she held the melting ice cream. Every single "oh," she pronounced, represented a beat of her heart. She felt paralyzed.

A doctor sat in his car and watched the young cop fighting with death. Maybe due to the incident he'd just witnessed, he felt woozy and couldn't move. He stared at the carnage as if his brain had shut down. After a couple of seconds, the doctor regained his composure and sprinted to the young cop. He applied pressure to the wounds to stop the bleeding while waiting for an ambulance. "God will save you," the doctor told the young cop in distress.

The young cop kept his hope high and stared at his daughter. In his mind, death would have to go through hell to take his life away because he wanted to avenge his daughter's merciless murder.

The doctor admired the young cop's will to live. Of course some people were crying, but many of them believed he would make it. An ambulance arrived on the scene and took him to the hospital. Since the young cop's wife couldn't maintain her composure, the doctor went to the hospital with the wounded officer.

Traffic on the way to the hospital represented their biggest challenge. The ambulance driver took the sidewalk, honked at the pedestrians and hit people's merchandise as he rushed to the nearest hospital. Those vendors cursed at him, but saving the life of the wounded cop was more important than any of their goods.

For Haitian citizens to occupy the sidewalks and sell their items while blaming the government for lack of space in the market for vendors had become normal. Therefore, pedestrians were at a higher risk of being hit by cars and bikes on the streets.

As the driver tried to avoid a big pot of boiling oil belonging to a woman who was selling all types of fried food, he got a flat tire. If the driver had hit the pot, the hot cooking oil would have been thrown into the air, burning many, and causing more injuries. The medical staff of the ambulance quickly replaced the tire and made it to the hospital, but too late. After about twenty-five minutes of fighting with death, the young cop succumbed to his injuries right at the hospital door. The medical team managed to resuscitate him, but in vain. His soul joined his daughter's.

The doctor and the ambulance staff glanced at each other. They felt sadness as they all realized another citizen had been added to the list of victims due to lack of infrastructure in the country. One of the medical staff in the ambulance couldn't hide his frustration. He clinched his fist and punched the ambulance. "Fuck, we were so close to saving him."

The doctor glanced at the medical staff, then the dead body, and said, "*C'est la vie.*"

Johanne's mother finally found a little strength to take a few steps. She crossed the street in desolation, mumbling words, and still holding the cone from the melted ice cream. She kneeled next to her daughter, held her in her arms, and screamed out of her unbearable pain, a pain one million times worse than what she'd felt while giving natural birth to her beautiful daughter. The gun was still next to Johanne on the ground when her mother took her in her embrace.

She kissed the bloody face of the girl and kept repeating, "Jo, don't do this to me. Wake up, baby!" She kept rocking Johanne. "Here's the ice cream, baby. Please wake up." She grabbed the gift from the ground and put it on Johanne's chest. "Here's your gift from your daddy. Open it, baby." In denial, the mother couldn't accept the demise of her daughter.

With those words, men, women, and children wept. Everyone felt the pain. They left Paul alone on the sidewalk as though his dead body didn't exist. Everyone surrounded the young woman in agony from her unimaginable loss. When the cops came, they couldn't find the words to comfort Johanne's mother.

A man from the mortuary came, covered Paul's body with a white sheet, and put it into the back of the mortuary van. He wanted to take Johanne's body, but her mother yelled, "Today is her birthday, and I didn't celebrate with her yet."

The mortuary worker insisted on taking the dead body of the little girl. Money was all he cared about. The citizens became angry and wanted to tear him to pieces. The cops didn't want him to face the wrath of the crowd. They suggested he wait and give the mother some time.

The doctor took a cab back to the crime scene to get his car. As soon as he got out of the cab, people asked him if the young cop had made it. He looked at them with his lips compressed and shook his head as tears rolled down his cheeks.

At that moment, Marjorie, Johanne's mother, a twenty-eight year old woman, understood her world had come to an end. Without her husband and her daughter, she had no reason to live anymore. She grabbed her husband's gun and put a bullet in her head. That afternoon hadn't stopped shocking people.

Sinking in despair from that dreadful tragedy like everybody else, the cops had forgotten to follow police protocol. They even forgot to ask for the guns of the two dead officers. Fortunately for these policemen, they worked in a poor country. Otherwise, Marjorie's family would have sued them for negligence.

Robert, the young cop, Johanne's father, had just turned thirty years old three months ago. Only the afterlife could tell if Robert and Marjorie were still celebrating Johanne's birthday or cursing out the man who took their lives away too soon.

The next day, the entire population became angry when the TV and radio broadcasted news of the incident. Many protested in the streets and asked for justice. Some rallied in front of the main building of MINUSTAH. The protesters requested the departure of the United Nations soldiers who failed to maintain peace within the country.

"Leave our country, thieves... Leave our country, kidnappers," the demonstrators clamored in the streets holding signs in their hands. The citizens claimed that the MINUSTAH were doing no good for the country. They knew that the last time they'd had foreign troops on Haitian soil was in 1995 and the soldiers were American. Those soldiers not only provided security during their time in Haiti, but they also built bridges and roads. Meanwhile MINUSTAH soldiers were involved in some cases of rape. People also saw it as an outrage to have foreign soldiers in Haiti to provide security for the country when they could have their own army doing the job.

Later that afternoon, Ronald's phone rang.

"Have you lost your mind? Why did you kill that little girl?" the captain asked.

"I won't stop until my brother is released," Ronald replied without remorse.

The captain understood he'd signed a contract with a ruthless man to whom life had no meaning. "You have to be patient. I'm working on his case and your actions just make the situation more difficult."

"Those motherfuckers should have never touched my brother."

"Remember we have a deal. You have to follow my orders."

"My brother being locked up wasn't part of the deal."

"I know… But there was nothing I could do. Just bad luck."

"Fix it," Ronald said before he hung up the phone.

Born into a poor family, Ronald came to earth as a joyful, nice, and sociable kid, but that soon changed. His father and mother left home early in the morning and returned late at night. Ronald raised himself and became a second father to his little brother. Some neighbors found it amusing to bully Ronald, a child of five years old bathing his little brother. Most of the time, many parts of Claude's body didn't come into contact with the water. They called Ronald *half and half* or *bathe a side, leave a side.*

Unable to wait for the return of his parents, Ronald ended up stealing food to feed himself and his brother. It became a habit for anyone who lost something to say Ronald had stolen it and complain to his father, who whipped the boy in return. Those whippings were no joke. His father beat him with a hammer when he couldn't find the electric cord that he used to discipline Ronald. Many felt saddened to look at all the slashes on Ronald's legs and back. Sometimes, before the wounds were healed, Ronald received another punishment.

Many Haitian parents misunderstood the difference between discipline and brutality. Their ancestors had rebelled against inhumane treatment and freed themselves from the French oppressors. Yet many Haitians remained slaves mentally and saw violence as the only way to bring about change within the society. The electric cord left so many scars on Ronald's body that he had to cover them with tattoos to escape the effect of his horrible childhood.

Ronald's father died an honest man. He carried his last name with pride beyond measure. From cleaning latrines to selling sugar cane, he did any type of hard work to earn a living, and wanted his children to grow up to be good citizens. However, he barely interacted with his sons, and never knew how much Ronald loved him.

Ronald's father, like many Haitians parents, believed food and education represented the only needs of a child. Understanding a child's behavior meant nothing. Through whipping, they thought a child would become a better person. Counseling was strictly reserved for adults.

Love is a seed already planted in everyone's heart, but it needs to be watered with love to produce love.

Ronald's heart was flooded with brutality from his father and hatred from his neighbors.

It's Fixed

Ten days after my first encounter with Miriam, on a Sunday morning around eleven-fifteen on my way home from church, I saw her once again. We greeted each other and then she asked, "Did you pray for me, neighbor?"

"Yes, indeed," I replied.

"What did you say in your prayer?"

"I said, thank you God for giving me the blessing of living next to an angel and being able to admire her beauty with my sinful eyes."

Miriam smiled and said, "Thank you… By the way, my TV is broken. Can you take a look at it for me, please?"

"Sure, no problem, neighbor."

When I walked in, I saw Judith, Miriam's niece, who Junior had a crush on, sitting on the floor and staring at the TV screen that showed static. I looked behind the TV; the cable that linked the TV to the antenna was disconnected. "Can you fix it?" Miriam asked me.

"I'll try my best," I replied.

I made the connection, and the TV displayed images once again, but of poor quality. I switched the position of the antenna a couple of times to get a better reception, yet the images didn't meet our expectations. Through a picture frame, I saw Miriam smiling at me as I moved the antenna. I wondered what she had in mind. Nevertheless, I found the house a bit quiet. "Where's your mother?" I asked.

"Monalisa has a grocery store at Cote Plage 18. She'll come back around five p.m.," Miriam replied.

"That's a beautiful name."

"I know, right. We call her Mona."

"Nice." I wished that name was hers instead. Monalisa sounded sexy and romantic.

"Judith, go on the roof to turn the antenna. I'll let you know when it's fixed," Miriam ordered.

In Haiti, the majority of TVs used two antennas: one they placed on top of the TV and the other one, made of aluminum, they put on the roof of the house. No need for a special device to access the local channels—all free.

Miriam shouted, "Judith, turn it right... No, left... No, turn it again, but slowly..." As Judith started turning the antenna in almost all directions, the TV began to display clearer images. "Stop, stop, it's fixed," Miriam yelled when the images came into focus.

Miriam thanked me and asked me if I wanted to stay a little while longer. I accepted her invitation. Judith went into the kitchen. In Haiti, it was considered very disrespectful for a child or a teenager to sit around adults who were having a conversation. We sat on the sofa and had a little chat about our religious beliefs and personal preferences in life. She confessed her love for the Transformers movies, a series that I'd enjoyed watching as cartoons during my childhood.

"Gotta go now," I said thirty minutes later.

"Already?"

"Yes, I'm a bit sleepy."

"You have an appointment with a girl." Miriam nodded.

I smiled, shook my head, and didn't add a single word. Deep inside, I wanted to stay, but I kept playing the *hard-to-get game*, cat-and-mouse, in which she would have to do the chasing.

When I left, I saw some of my male friends from the neighborhood sitting on a wall in front of Miriam's house. They looked shocked at seeing me close the door behind me. I waved at them. One of them shouted, "Leito, luckiest player." They all laughed out loud, and another one added, "I wish I could be you."

I shook my head and continued my walk toward my house. Anytime I spoke to a woman, many thought I'd had sex with her or soon would. I heard them whispering about me, but I didn't bother to find out their comments or thoughts.

Since the majority of Haitians were jobless, in almost all neighborhoods in Port-au-Prince you found young men sitting on walls and observing every single thing. I guessed it represented a way for some to escape depression. Imagine a thirty-four-year-old man who'd never worked one day in his life and still depended on his parents.

That night, Jean-Baptiste told me that they'd transferred him to Jérémie, the capital city of the Grand'Anse department in Haiti for the next six months.

The next evening, on my way back from dropping off one of my girls, I saw Miriam and her mother sitting on chairs on the porch of their house.

"Neighbor, come sit with us, and tell us some jokes," Miriam said.

"Leave him alone. He's not a comedian," Mona replied.

"You never know, Mom," Miriam countered.

"It's late. Let's go to bed."

"It's only nine-thirty," Miriam replied.

"I know, but I'm going to sleep very soon," Mona added.

"Okay, your bed is ready. You can go anytime. I'm not sleepy yet."

"Okay, neighbor, I'll stay for a few minutes, but not too long," I said to end the discussion.

"That's fine with me," Miriam said.

I took a seat next to Miriam and told her a few jokes before I went home.

After that night, Junior and I stopped by Miriam's almost every night to hang out with her. I redirected all the attention onto Junior instead of me. Junior entertained them with many jokes, and I smiled more than I talked. If I had to say something, I made sure it came out concise and precise. As the nights went by, Junior and I created a humorous and friendly environment. Nine-fifteen p.m. became our meeting time in front of Miriam's house. However, as hard as we tried to make Mona laugh with our jokes, she remained cold and forced herself to smile.

Aside from her pit bull attitude toward any man who tried to approach her or her daughter, Mona was a beautiful black woman with low, thick eyebrows. She had long curly black hair with the most succulent breasts I ever seen—size 38 double D. Her four foot, ten inches didn't take anything away from her voluptuousness. She loved hoop earrings and wore a heart necklace all the time—her husband's last gift to her before he passed away.

Mona stated that her husband was the first and would be the last man to know her till the day she died. Many men perceived Mona as a wild woman who needed a virile man to tame her and help her release all her anger. She hadn't been with a man for more than fifteen years. Addiction or attachment, Mona never started her day without a cup of hot, dark, sweetened Haitian coffee, freshly brewed.

The 3D Team

Miriam had two best friends: Elizabeth and Rachelle. Elizabeth was leaving the country for Canada the next morning. A few friends gathered at a lounge to wish her luck. Miriam asked me to accompany her.

As soon as we stepped into the lounge, Elizabeth stood up and hugged Miriam and then me. Elizabeth had met me before when she'd visited Miriam's new place. So she introduced me to everyone else as Miriam's friend. "Leito, this is Appolon, my boyfriend. This is Jeanne, Sofia, and Rachelle."

I greeted each person with a handshake before I took a seat at the table. Everyone was dressed casually. I had on black slim-fit jeans, a white Lacoste t-shirt, and black and white Puma sneakers.

Rachelle grabbed my attention right away. She looked stunning with her big, beautiful, hazel eyes. She wore white pants with a yellow blouse and yellow heels. I fought hard to not glance at her too much, but I couldn't help it. To my surprise, Rachelle did the same thing back.

Although Elizabeth was the main reason for our presence in the lounge, somehow I became the attraction of the party for the others, who wanted to get to know me a bit: my taste, my profession, my study, etc.... Within under two hours, the table was littered with empty glasses and bottles of beer and sodas. The ladies knew how to handle their alcohol.

"A toast to the 3D Team," Appolon said after rising up with a glass of wine in his hand.

"To the 3D Team," the rest of us shouted in chorus.

Elizabeth, Rachelle, and Miriam had grown up together in the same neighborhood, in Cote Plage 22, and went to the same high school. Their professor of literature gave them the nickname the 3D Team, which meant three dynamites, diamonds, and divas. Many found it intriguing that three single, beautiful women had gotten along for so many years without fighting over a man.

Always together, they followed the same rule, honesty. Their beauty created such a confidence that once in a while they liked to stroll down the streets with short skirts to harass men. Some people labeled them lesbians, a speculation made because the three women were friendly with everyone and not accessible to all the men in their neighborhoods. Many loved to invent stories and conjecture when they had no clue about something or someone. Meanwhile, they could have simply asked a question and received an answer.

"Is Leito your boyfriend?" Rachelle asked Miriam.

I looked at Rachelle and wondered what she had in mind.

"Green light," Elizabeth replied with a grin.

The answer satisfied Rachelle, who smiled from ear to ear. "Leito is a cupcake, girls... A sweet dessert," she said before she handed me her cell phone. "Put in your number. I'll be in touch with you shortly." Rachelle always spoke her mind.

I glanced at Miriam, and she gave me a wry smile before I entered my cell phone number. I represented a cupcake to Rachelle because I was twenty-five years old, six feet tall, single with no kids, working as a bank teller, and handsome with a great future ahead. Whenever I said I worked as a teller at the best commercial bank in Haiti, it amazed people. I got paid forty-two-hundred Gourdes, about one-hundred-and-five US dollars every two weeks, and people thought I swam in money.

The boyfriends of those three women ranged from forty-five years old and up. Elizabeth, Rachelle, and Miriam followed one principle—be with men who could meet their financial needs, until they found a Romeo who could take over financially and sexually. The three friends often complained to each other about their unhappiness because most of the time their boyfriends were married. Quite often, the men they loved didn't have enough time to take care of them.

Many women in Haiti had become the sole earners of income for their entire families. Some parents pushed their sons to go beyond high school in their education and let their daughters only finish high school. They believed every woman was born with a treasure between her legs.

In a country where having a job was actually a luxury, women from low-income families found themselves caught between two choices: live in misery or in some form of degradation that included being with a thief or a married man, or sleeping with a manager to get a job—and taking all the risks that came with it. As the Haitian maxim says, "Beautiful women don't suffer." Rachelle viewed me as her way out.

Miriam became angry and refused to look at me. Seeing me smile at Rachelle obviously made her feel uncomfortable. Miriam was the most beautiful, but Rachelle was the most seductive women on the 3D Team. With her five-foot, ten-inch frame, long legs, flat belly, and sexy body, she looked like a model.

Rachelle had to leave early. "Leito, do you mind walking me out?" Rachelle asked me.

I nodded before I stood up and followed her. Once outside, Rachelle turned and walked toward me. Before I knew it, her nose touched mine, and we were breathing each other's air. She kept moving, and I walked backward as I tried to figure out her true intention. My back hit the wall of the lounge, and she pressed her sexy body against mine. Rachelle stared at me for a few seconds, and her hazel eyes told me, *There's no escape, Leito.*

Rachelle kissed me as though she wanted to rape me. I needed a couple of seconds to react as she caught me off guard. I grabbed her derriere and squeezed. My penis started rising in my boxers. Rachelle pulled herself away from me. She looked at me, bit her bottom lip, and then shook her head. "Leito, Leito."

Let's go to my house and finish it, I wanted her to say. Rachelle's house was two blocks away from the lounge. But she turned around and walked away without saying goodbye. "Damn it! She's provocative," I muttered.

As I admired the sway of her hips in those high heels as she edged away, dirty thoughts invaded my mind. I wanted to fuck Rachelle so hard that she would have to change the way she walked for days. Some women called me "Beast. I told them they should have never messed around with a Capricorn, half human, half animal. Yet those women craved my animalistic skills in bed. They told me they loved to wake up the next day and not be able to wash—their labia majora and minora too sore to be touched. I loved to tattoo my name inside of them. Whenever someone says sex, my name should come up first in their mind.

I also pictured Rachelle kneeling in front on me with her mouth open and her tongue out. I would grip her hair, hold my torch and turn it into a whip, and then smack it on her tongue until her tongue became numb. Rachelle needed to be taught to keep her tongue inside and not tease the Beast.

I closed my eyes to shut down my nasty imagination and then sighed. I inserted my right hand inside my pocket and grabbed my erect and disappointed phallus before I walked back inside. I didn't want anyone to glance at my pants and guess about those minutes I'd spent outside with Rachelle.

The rest of us left the lounge around eleven p.m. Aside from Miriam, we'd all had a great time at the lounge. Miriam and I didn't say much to each other. She was angry at me, and I was thinking about Rachelle.

Elizabeth's boyfriend gave us a ride back home. He dropped Jeanne and Sofia off first and then Miriam and me.

Once we got out of the car, we hugged Elizabeth once again and wished her luck on her new beginning.

Standing at five-foot, seven-inches tall with a caramel complexion and short, black hair, Elizabeth was the most stylish and charming member of the 3D Team. She spoke with a slight lisp. She had the most beautiful smile, and her teeth were white as snow. Her cat-shaped eyes earned her the nickname of "Kitty Cat." She had the biggest derriere among the three friends. They also called her "Neck Breaker." When she walked by or stood up, men broke their necks to glance at her.

Elizabeth called Miriam to the side and said to her, "I saw what happened. You don't need to tell me. I observed you a lot tonight. You have a thing for Leito. Why did you lie to me?" Although I had my head down as if not listening to their talk, I heard almost every word.

Miriam sighed. "I didn't lie. Leito is just a friend, but…"

"You know our rule. If you want him, go for it. Don't wait. You know Rachelle."

Miriam nodded, hugged Elizabeth, and said, "I'll miss you."

"If you had listened to me, we would have been going together tomorrow," Elizabeth told her.

"I know, but I can't leave Mom behind by herself," Miriam said in a guilty tone.

"I understand Mona is your mom, and you're her only child. You have to live your life, baby. I think she'll understand. Finally, I feel free," Elizabeth countered.

"What do you mean?"

"I have no clue what's waiting for me in Canada. But one thing I know for sure, I'm going to a country where I don't need to rely on a man for everything and will be able to live with a man I can call mine."

With a nod, Miriam acknowledged the truth of Elizabeth's statement. "Finally Appolon agreed to let you go."

"He hasn't spoken to me for three weeks. I'm surprised he came out tonight," Elizabeth replied.

Miriam nodded. "They're all the same. They have their own families and keep us as their side chicks. Whenever we want to move on with our lives, they throw a chain around our necks."

"One more thing, remember Raul is a mad, jealous man. Be careful," warned Elizabeth.

"I should be the one telling you about him. I deal with the man," Miriam said.

A few seconds later, Mona came out in pajamas and said to Miriam, "Oh, I thought you went to Canada."

"What do you mean, Mona?" Elizabeth asked as she frowned.

"Oh! It's almost midnight, and Miriam knows I have to lock my doors."

"Sorry, Mom—we didn't see the time passing that fast."

"Anyway… I wish you all the best and please don't listen to friends to put yourself in trouble. You're going to a foreign country. Please behave and make me proud of you," Mona advised Elizabeth.

"Thank you. Don't worry about me because all my best friends are in Haiti," Elizabeth stated before she hugged Mona.

Mona bent near the driver's window to look at the driver and then said, "Appolon, I know you're always drunk when you're driving. Please, drop Elizabeth home safe and sound."

"She's in good hands. I only had two beers tonight," Appolon replied.

Elizabeth and Miriam glanced at each other after that statement from Appolon. They raised their eyebrows and nodded. He'd almost finished a bottle of Rhum Barbancourt by himself.

Appolon was fifty-six years old, a nice and friendly man, married to a Haitian woman who lived in Boston with his three kids. He'd come to Haiti and opened a hardware store. His family visited him once a year, and he flew frequently to Boston to spend time with them. Addicted to alcohol and young women, he always wanted to show off his capability to drink a lot of alcohol, even though doctors had diagnosed him with cirrhosis of the liver. Appolon stated that doctors had diagnosed his father with the same disease when his father was thirty years old, and yet his father had died at seventy-three. Appolon believed his body had developed some sort of tolerance for alcohol.

Mona, Miriam, and I waved goodbye to Elizabeth before she got back into the car and left with Appolon.

"I hope you don't do that again," Mona admonished before she slammed the door behind her and entered the house.

"Thank you for coming with me tonight," Miriam said as she struggled to hide her emotion.

"You're welcome, my dear. It was a pleasure. I had a lot fun tonight."

"I can tell."

I hugged Miriam and watched her enter her house before I went home. I couldn't wait to see Rachelle again, and early the next morning, I received the following text message from her: Not only do you look and smell good, your lips are soft and sweet. From that day on, Rachelle and I stayed connected over the phone.

Proof of Love

As the nights went by, more eyes focused on Miriam and me. She was an angel, and I was a star. Many desired my position—close to her.

"Neighbor, can I sit next to you?" Maurice asked Miriam.

"Why?" Mona replied as she raised her eyebrows.

"I see Leito and Junior telling jokes, so... I wanted to join the crowd."

"We don't have a public place here, and if you think it's a theater, then it's full," Mona said. With a thousand wrinkles in her forehead, Mona looked like a tiger ready to attack. Embarrassed and scared, Maurice walked away.

Mona cared a lot about her daughter's reputation. She heard how men within the neighborhood talked about women they had a dalliance with, so she didn't want her daughter to suffer the same fate. Since Junior and I behaved well and showed no romantic interest during our conversations with Miriam, Mona became a bit flexible with us.

"How many black and white t-shirts do you have, neighbor?" Miriam asked.

"Leito has a lot. That's all he wears," Junior replied.

I had some clothes, but I didn't use them too much. I wore them for special occasions. It made more sense for me to buy a dozen of those V-neck white or black t-shirts for less than two US dollars and wear them on a daily basis. I projected a look of simplicity; in reality, I tried to spend less on unnecessary things and invest more in my education. I was enrolled in a certified public accounting prep test that had cost an arm and a leg.

When Miriam knew I spoke English as well, she started to use it in our discussions. She was also taking English classes. Miriam and I wanted to get to know each other a bit more. So here and there, we used English as a shield to protect our conversation and to prevent interference from others.

"Tell me a little bit about you," Miriam said in English.

"Like what?" I asked.

"Who you are, your goals in life, and beliefs?"

"I believe in God. I love soccer, and I always smile regardless of the situation."

"No need to tell. You're always happy," Miriam said.

"When I'm sick I don't tell anyone."

"Why?" Miriam asked.

"I don't know. I just don't want to bother others."

"When someone needs your help, do you feel that you're being bothered?"

"No, it's not the case. I love to help people."

"You should tell somebody when you're not feeling well, because it could cause your death one day. You never know," she advised me.

"You're right. Also I hate when people wake me up for nothing and... I get angry too quickly."

I could have stated all my good qualities to Miriam, but I felt she would be more interested in me if I came out as sounding sincere. Also I wanted to know where I could fail. I'd met many women, but none like Miriam. She had a different mentality.

"What about you?" I asked.

"I like people who are clean, smell good, and are smart, and respectful."

"That's good."

"I don't like to forgive people. I feel they already know what they shouldn't do."

"We're humans, we make mistakes. Forgiveness is a proof of love," I said.

"One more thing, I hate liars. Tell me the truth, regardless. Don't tell me I look like the moon. I don't. Be humble enough to tell me exactly what you have in mind."

"I agree with you."

"Do you have a lot of friends?" Miriam asked.

"I call everyone friend, but I differentiate between people I know and those who are really my friends. A friend is someone you love, a person you can trust with your secrets, and someone who will be there for you in good or bad moments."

"Do you wanna be my friend?" Miriam asked.

"I'd love too."

"You know that's disrespectful to speak a foreign language when other people are here," Mona said.

Deep in our conversation, Miriam and I had forgotten about everyone else around us. We didn't realize that Mona, Judith, and Junior hadn't spoken a word for about fifteen minutes. They stared at us, obviously feeling left out.

"Raul doesn't want me to go to study group. Now I found Leito to practice my English with, you don't want it," Miriam replied.

"I didn't say I don't want it. I said you should have waited till I'm not around," Mona said.

"When are you not around?" Miriam asked in an irritated voice.

Sorry Mona, we simply want to get better at the language. I thought about saying that, but I kept my mouth shut. I didn't want to interfere in family business and I feared that Mona would say something that would have hurt my feelings.

"This is my fault I put you in school. Now you feel I'm too low for you," Mona added.

"What do you and Raul want me to do?" Miriam asked her mother as she stood up before she walked inside the house. She slammed the door behind her. Judith and Mona followed Miriam. I glanced at Junior, and we left.

"Player, don't mess up what we've accomplished so far," Junior said to me when we got home.

Before I went to bed, Miriam called me and apologized for her behavior.

Just Do It

The following night, Mona entered the house a bit early and left us alone.

"You're shy, neighbor," Miriam said.

"Not really," I replied.

"Yes, you are. Look at me in the eyes."

As I tried to avoid eye contact with her, Miriam lifted my chin and looked me in the eyes. With my eyes semi-closed, I glanced at her and smiled. If only she had an inkling about the effect of my eyes on women. My big brown eyes worked like magnets that made people's attention gravitate toward me. My grandmother had the best definition of me. She said that I was a lion with the appearance of a lamb.

A few minutes later, I stood up and wished Miriam good night. She gave me a bemused look as she no doubt wondered at the reason behind my early departure. Miriam probably thought she'd made me uncomfortable with her statement of my being shy. The following night, I did the same thing when Mona went inside.

"What are you doing, player? Whenever Mona goes inside, you leave. Why?" Junior asked me on the second night before I entered my room.

"Relax, man, I got this," I replied.

"I hope you know what you're doing."

"Tomorrow, when Mona leaves, go around her house and look through her living room window."

"Why?"

"Just do it," I replied.

The next day, Junior did as I asked him. He went by Mona's living room window after she left us on the porch. He came back and said, "Leito, let's go. Good night, ladies."

Confused, Miriam glanced at Junior and me. She found our behavior weird, no doubt, but she didn't question us. She must have thought we would have been happy and stayed longer after her mother went inside.

When Junior went to look through the living room window, he'd spotted Mona eyeballing Miriam and me. Mona monitored every single action we made and every word that came out of our mouths. To get to Miriam, I knew I had to build trust within her mother. By leaving a few minutes after she went, I created in Mona's mind the illusion that I had no romantic interest in her daughter.

"Leito, respect. How did you know?" Junior asked me when we reached home.

"Last week, a friend of Miriam's came by, and I spotted her doing that."

"I would have never thought of it."

"She's on the lookout," I said.

"Anyway, ten minutes is too short for me," Junior said.

"Be quicker, player."

Since Miriam and I couldn't speak English as we wished, I came up with a new strategy to confess my sentiment—music.

"Do you know that song?" I asked Miriam.

"Which one?" she replied.

I sang to her the chorus of the song's lyrics, When I Dream at Night.

As a smart woman, she understood my code, and she said, "That's Marc Anthony. I really love this song. Do you want to know the one I like?"

"Tell me," I said.

Miriam sang to me the first verse of Dreaming of You by Selena.

I asked Mona about her favorite song. She mentioned many songs from a Haitian band named Orchestre Tropicana d'Haiti. Anytime I asked Miriam a question, I asked her mother the same question to make Mona feel at ease. I didn't have to worry about Junior and Judith.

That night, instead of just a "good night, neighbor," Miriam hugged me. The music strategy worked for us. We stuck to it the following nights. We used Haitian Compa songs, French romantic songs, Spanish songs—any song that could reveal what we felt inside. Music helped our friendship grow faster and better.

One night, all five of us were sitting in front on the porch and talking about the most beautiful places to visit in Haiti. Miriam said, "Neighbor, can you help me reach something in the living room? It's too high for me."

"Leave him alone. Why don't you use a chair?" Mona replied before I even answered her daughter.

"Mom, why should I use a chair when I could use his height?"

"Or wait for Raul tomorrow," Mona said.

Miriam glanced at her mother. Mona just shook her head. Miriam leaned forward, took my hand, and walked toward the living room with me. As soon I stepped in the living room, Miriam pulled me into a corner, cupped my face in her hands, and kissed me. A quick and the most passionate kiss I ever had from a woman. I took her in my embrace and squeezed her body against mine. I desired to kiss her more, but I didn't want her mother to suspect anything.

"Where's the thing you want me to help you with?" I asked.

"I just had what I wanted," Miriam replied before she smiled.

Miriam and I walked back outside as though nothing had happened.

From that moment on, many things changed. Miriam no longer called me "neighbor," she used my name. I called her "Angel"—in the absence of her mother. When I told jokes that she loved, Miriam poked me or leaned on my shoulder. The more we kissed, the more open and free we became with each other.

Side Chick

A few days later, in the afternoon, many of my friends including Junior were sitting on a wall in front of Miriam's porch and talking about soccer and women as usual. Raul parked his car in front of them and got out with a revolver attached to his waist.

"I heard some of you are enjoying the pleasure of coming and courting my wife every night. Ask about me just in case you don't know who I am. I would murder for my wife. I don't play," Raul said before he entered Miriam's house.

All the men looked at each other and remained stunned following Raul's warning. When I got home from work, Junior reported Raul's statement to me and advised me to give up on the Miriam quest.

"I'm not gonna let Zacchaeus kill me for a woman. My life is more important. If you want to continue to see Miriam that's your choice," Junior said. He nicknamed Raul, Zacchaeus because he was short like the tax collector in the Bible.

"Punk, you're scared. Your stomach must be clenching right now," I joked.

"It's not about being scared. You only live once, player. Life is too beautiful for me to put it at stake for a woman."

"What about Judith?" I asked.

"If she had given me the cookie, I would stay. Anyway, there's plenty of cats out there to chase. I'm good player." When Junior saw Raul's gun, he'd freaked out.

In poor countries, money was might. People like Raul could get away with many things. With their finances and influence, they bent the justice system as they wished. They hired bandits to kill for them. Rumor or fact, a few stories about Raul's power had disseminated within the neighborhood. He was a director at a private, prestigious high school in the city and had good connections with the government and politicians.

"Tonight might be my last meeting with you," I said to Miriam later on when we sat on her porch.

"Why?"

"Your husband said that he's ready to kill for you."

"Husband?" Miriam asked as she raised her eyebrows.

I shrugged, and pretended I didn't know anything about her private life.

"Raul has a wife and three kids at home. I'm just a side chick," Miriam said.

I liked Miriam for her honesty. She had no shame in calling herself a side chick.

"What should I do then?" I asked her.

"I'm the reason you're here. I'll let you know when you should no longer come."

I felt no fear, and Raul didn't represent a threat to me. I listened to Miriam's comment and continued to meet with her every night without Junior.

Go Back to Sleep

On a Saturday morning, I was cleaning my bedroom and noticed the shadow of someone standing by the door. I turned my head and saw Miriam observing me. She wore a yellow t-shirt and short jeans. I only had boxers on.

"That's good you know how to clean," she said.

"Thanks," I replied.

"What else can you do?" Miriam asked.

"I can cook and do laundry."

"So you're a well-prepared man."

"Kind of."

"I'll call you when I'm cleaning my house," she added.

"Anytime."

Miriam removed her flip-flops at the door and walked on the red rug I had on the floor. As she entered, she slid her fingertips on top of my CD player that rested on a small table. She looked at her fingertips and then said, "You clean well."

"Thank you," I replied.

"You need a bookshelf," Miriam said when she glanced at all my books lined up on the side of my bed against the wall.

"I'm thinking about buying one."

"What kind of ceremony were you doing here?" she asked after looking over my room.

"It's a secret," I replied as I juggled with Miriam's curiosity, hoping she would ask me about the secret. She did not.

"No chair, mattress on the floor, four candle holders filled with wax, bottles of wine, two glasses... What kind of room... never mind. Give me a knife so I can clean the candle holders for you," Miriam said as she shook her head in disbelief.

"Give me a second. Let me go get one in the kitchen."

"Keep in mind, I don't work for free."

"I will pay you, don't worry," I said.

"I hope so," she answered before she smiled.

I went into the kitchen and brought a knife back to Miriam. She cleared the wax from the candle holders.

By removing the chairs, laying my mattress on the rug, and having bottles of wine, I set up a trap for women. Any woman who entered the room had to sit on the mattress. By the time she sipped some wine, she found herself lying flat on my bed, which eased my job. Given the candlelight and the walls painted in sky blue, the room looked homey.

Since I couldn't rely on electricity in the country, I loaded my radio with batteries to play only romantic songs—pre-selected. I didn't like improvisation, so I planned my questions in advance and had the expected answers in my mind. Any word, any move, any smile, any joke was perfectly planned. Many called me "Player", but I believed they should have called me "Gamer" or "The Architect"—I made plays and reinvented the game.

Once done with the cleaning, I sprinted to the bathroom and took a shower. Upon my return, I glanced in astonishment at my room—Miriam had rearranged it. She'd done such a good job that I felt as though she'd bought me a new bedroom.

Miriam had placed the mattress in the middle of the room. She'd lined up the books on the left side of the room against the wall. She put the radio on the rug in a corner and put one bottle of wine on the small table with two glasses. She stuck the other bottles inside a drawer in my dresser. She put my watches and colognes on top of my dresser as if she were displaying them for sale.

"Wow, thank you. How much do I owe you now?" I asked.

"Pay me with sweet kisses."

I motioned toward her, twirled my fingers in her belt loop, and thrust her against me. She caressed my back while I kissed her lips and then her neck. As we shared that sweet and passionate moment, my torch rose, and I tried to pull her pants down. She looked at me, put her right palm on my chest to create a space between us, and said, "Not now," as she shook her head.

I swooshed like a truck and exhaled all the pressure I had in me. The towel fell on the floor. I stood up naked in front of her. She grabbed my torch, shook it in a handshake manner, and then said to it, "Go back to sleep," before she landed a soft kiss on my chest and left.

Miriam had teased me and left me hanging. I stood in the middle of my room and dreamt about all the things I could have done with her. More blood flowed in my phallus, and I felt a strong need to ejaculate. Too bad for me, I never practiced masturbation. I picked up my phone and called Emma, one of the girls I was messing with.

Emma came a few minutes later. She helped me release that pressure and saved me from blue balls.

When Junior came home, I told him that Miriam had surprised me with a visit.

"She came to the clinic, player?" Junior asked.

"Yep, she did."

"What happened? Did she have a consultation?"

"No, man, she didn't stay long."

Junior called my room "the Clinic" because women came and left. Every month a new face showed up, added to those who were already there. The majority of the women I slept with couldn't claim me as boyfriend. I never gave them the girlfriend title.

Miriam left me wanting more. We continued to have romantic moments at her house, and still no access to her cookie jar. I started losing my patience. To know where I stood, I wrote her the following quiz.

1-Chose the correct answer

    a)   I love you

    b)   You love me

    c)   We love each other

2-Complete the following sentence

    a)   In   my   presence,   you feel...

b)   When we're alone, you like to

....

c)   The things you love about me

are:...

d)   You would like me to make love to

you with............... So........................

The next day on my way home from work, I beheld Miriam standing in front of her porch, apparently waiting for me. She wore a slim-leg black and white plaid print dress pants and a white top. When I got closer, before I even greeted her, Miriam dipped her left hand into her back pocket, pulled out a sheet of paper, and handed it to me—the quiz I had given her. When I reached home, I opened the letter where she'd filled out the blanks with the following words.

1-Chose the correct answer

a)   I love you

b)   You love me

c)   <u>We love each other</u>

2-Complete the following sentence

a)   In my presence, you feel: loved, comfortable, and at peace.

b)   When we're alone, you like to: kiss you.

c)   The things you love about me are: your eyes, your discretion, your kindness, your ability to reason, your honesty and your great sense of humor.

e)   You would like me to make love to you with............tenderness... So.........we must wait.

P.S: keep in mind; I'm not a big fan of writing letters.

Later on, I asked her about how long I would have to wait to make love to her. She told me that she liked me very much, but she didn't feel ready. Since Miriam appeared undecided, I switched to Rachelle, and Miriam became priority number two.

Do You Love Me?

On a Saturday, early in the afternoon, Miriam called and asked me to come over to her house to help her with a chapter in Accounting Principles that she hadn't understood well in class. Miriam had struggled with that class since she rejected her professor who wanted to have a love affair with her. He was trying his best to fail her, but Miriam was determined to pass the class.

I went by Miriam's house where I sat down next to her on the sofa in the living room. She leaned forward and pulled the living room table closer to us and put the accounting book on it. I explained the chapter to her. I used some copy paper to practice some exercises. She impressed me with her quick understanding of the material. I loved working with smart and dedicated people.

Once we finished, Miriam started looking at the pictures on my phone, a Nokia 7650. A few seconds later, the phone rang, and she threw it at my chest. I caught it, smiled, and wondered why she threw it at me. When I looked at the screen, it was Rachelle calling. I said to myself, *Damn it*!

I answered the call and walked outside. Miriam tried to play it cool like she was unbothered. As soon as I came back into the living room, Miriam said, "Done so quick."

I could tell she was being sarcastic. So, I glanced at my watch and replied, "I was on the phone for about twenty minutes."

"Yeah, right, it was more like an hour. What were you and Rachelle talking about for so long?" Miriam asked as she rolled her eyes.

"Nothing special," I replied as I shrugged.

"Hmm…"

I understood Miriam, but I couldn't afford to lose both women. Miriam had advised me to be patient with her. Meanwhile, Rachelle told me she liked me and looked forward to growing a relationship with me. As I was about to give my phone back to Miriam, it rang again. "Put the phone on speaker. I want to know what you're plotting with Rachelle."

I smiled and put the phone on speaker.

"Oh, I forgot to tell you I love you," Rachelle said.

Miriam stared at me and waited for my answer. In for a penny, in for a pound, "Love you too, honey," I replied.

My answer shocked Miriam. I could see her shaking. A few seconds later, water filled her eyes. Yet she managed to shed no tears. I gave my phone to her for a second time, and it slid out of her hand. "Sorry, my hands are sweaty," she apologized.

I took the phone off the floor, gave it to her, and then said, "It's okay. It's not broken."

Miriam held the phone tighter, and the tears finally rolled down her cheeks as she continued to look at my photo slideshow. "Are you okay?" I asked.

"Yeah, something just flew into my eyes, but I'm fine though," Miriam answered as she wiped her cheeks. She'd had an emotional breakdown. A few minutes later, she said, "I have a bad headache. I need to take a nap."

I hugged her, and she walked in a daze into her bedroom. Before I went back home, I stopped by a deli, bought some aspirin, and brought them to Miriam. She appreciated my care. I regretted being so naïve as to put the phone on speaker.

Around two a.m., my phone rang.

"What are you up to?" Miriam asked in English.

"Chillin," I replied.

"I thought you were sleeping."

"Not really," I lied as I yawned and tried to open my eyes.

"Can we talk?"

"Of course, I'm listening," I said as I cleared my throat.

"Do you love Rachelle?"

"I like Rachelle, but I want you."

"You don't have to lie to me. Be honest. I won't be mad at you."

"Rachelle makes my eyes blink. You make my heart pound."

"What will you do if Rachelle wants to have sex with you?" Miriam asked.

"Are you ready for the answer?"

"Spit it out."

"I would go for it," I said.

"Do you know if you do that I won't be able to be with you?"

"What do you mean?"

"That's our rule. None of us can sleep with the same guy."

"Wow."

"Yep, it's our vow."

"Do you love me?" I asked Miriam.

"Yes I do, but I'm not sure of you. I hear words, but I can't see your heart."

"I want to be with you, Miriam."

"You must say the same thing to Rachelle."

I spent almost two hours trying to convince Miriam about my love for her—my lust. However, she kept saying she couldn't trust me. I wanted her badly and was willing to do anything in my power to have sex with her.

"What do you want?" I asked her.

"I don't know."

"Wow. You know what. I can't force you to trust me. To make you happy, I'll forget about Rachelle."

"I didn't ask that."

"You didn't, but I think it will prove my love for you."

"How do you want me to trust you with my heart when I know you're sleeping with other girls?" Miriam asked.

"It's already four-twenty-five a.m. I want to sleep now," I snapped.

"I'd like to feel at ease when I speak to you, but sometimes it proves difficult. That doesn't mean I'm not willing to try."

"Have a good night."

"Good night," Miriam said in sorrow.

Once I hung up the phone, I yelled, "Fuck, fuck, fuck," as I punched my pillow three times. My impatience had caused me to perceive her as an annoying person. After I rolled over on my bed, I begged for sleep to rescue me from those mosquitoes that played a symphony in my ears and tried to show me love with their bites. With no electricity to help me cool off, I became even more upset. I kicked my pillow and threw my sheet. I rolled over back and forth on my bed until I fell asleep around six a.m.

Be Closer

On the evening of the following Saturday, Rachelle and I went to a restaurant called Pollo Caliente, a place well known for its barbeque and cocktails, situated less than a quarter mile from her house. We both ordered barbeque fish with fried green plantains and garden salad on the side. Rachelle and I enjoyed our dishes and spent a good time listening to some Haitian Compa songs while sipping on some Prestige, our favorite Haitian beer.

Once done, we strolled back home holding each other's hand instead of taking public transportation. Rachelle told me she was moving back to Jacmel, her hometown where she'd found a job with an international non-governmental organization. They'd hired her as a human resources assistant manager.

As we sauntered, I felt the need to urinate. I held it as long as I could, until I felt a burning sensation in my right kidney. I stopped by a tree, in the dark of course, and said, "I wanna pee."

"Do you want to explode?" Rachelle asked me.

"Yes, I do."

Rachelle bent in front of me, unzipped my slim-fit blue Levi jeans, pulled out my phallus, put it in her mouth, and the rest belonged to history. I never thought I would find myself doing something so crazy in the middle of the street. She didn't care about who could see her. I kept glancing everywhere and enjoyed the moment. Lucky us, no one came by.

"Did you like it?" Rachelle asked me as she stood up.

"I looooved it."

As fun as it sounded, my right kidney hurt me more when I tried to pee. I then felt great satisfaction and sighed when the urine started coming out my pipe. Having such a crazy experience was worth the discomfort.

When Rachelle and I arrived in front of her house, we kissed and wished each other a good night. On my way back home, I replayed that unbelievable moment in my head—she'd swallowed.

Since that marvelous night with Rachelle, I only stopped by Miriam's house every other day. I told Junior that I had to prepare for my CPA test and couldn't spend time every night with Miriam. Miriam understood that I'd started to avoid her as much as I could, but she called me more often to help her with her accounting class. I didn't deny her my knowledge and help, but once I was done, I went home.

"Why do you act like a stranger now?" Miriam asked me one day.

"What do you mean?"

"Lately, I feel something has changed with you. It seems as if you're giving me distance while I'm in your presence. Is this how you really are? Tell me what's wrong."

"I haven't changed."

"Yes, you have. You don't smile with me or gaze at me anymore," Miriam said.

"I respect your decision, and I can't torture my heart."

"I understand, but I'm afraid." Her eyes moistened.

"I can't argue with you on that. My behavior doesn't speak in my favor," I admitted.

"I understand your behavior based on what you've told me about your past relationships. You say you felt betrayed every time you gave your heart to someone. One day, I could feel differently about you, but I need you to be closer for me to be able to trust you."

"You're right," I said as I nodded.

"Will I see you tonight?"

I just looked at Miriam and didn't answer. She grabbed my arms, pulled me against her, landed my palms on her butt, and whispered in my ears, "I love the moment we look into each other's eyes, the warmth of your hugs when you hold me tight. Your kindness means more to me than you can imagine. I miss the nice and cool Leito."

I sighed and took her in my embrace before I went home.

When I entered my room, I jumped on my bed, and started thinking about Miriam. I put my hands beneath my head and stared at the ceiling as though it were a big flat-screen TV displaying my behavior. I saw that my pride and impatience had taken over so well I'd forgotten my absence wouldn't play in my favor in wining Miriam's trust. Deep inside, I knew having sex with her preoccupied my head more than the intention of gaining her heart. I wanted so badly to get the job done and write my name on the scoreboard. Now I listened to Miriam's advice, reviewed my plan, and again started my routine of meeting with her on the porch in front of her house.

Miriam showed a lot of interest in me after that. I came back stronger. Some days, I surprised her with a box of chocolates, or a greeting card. We took our friendship to another level. When Raul realized his threat hadn't stopped my friendship with Miriam, he started leaving her house late. However, Miriam did her best to see me regardless.

Commando

On a Sunday, around two p.m., Miriam visited me for a second time. I was lying on my bed and listening to some Haitian romantic songs when she walked in. She wore a light-blue denim buttoned-down shirt, dark blue jeans, and taupe wedge sandals that she removed at the door.

"How's your day going?" she asked as she leaned her back against the wall.

"So far, so good," I replied, and I rolled over to sit at the edge of the mattress.

"I love that song," she told me when the radio played "J'ai Besoin de Toi" by Alan Cave.

"Let's dance," I said. I stood up on the bed and leaned forward to take her hand.

Miriam climbed onto the bed, and we danced. She was about to get off the bed when the radio played the next song, "Mamacita" by Carimi, a Haitian band. "Oh no, I need to dance to that one," she said.

As our waists undulated against each other to the melody of the song, my adrenaline rose. Miriam slid her hands underneath my white V-neck t-shirt to caress my back, and I did the same, just to realize she had no bra on. I did my best to reach her boobs and rolled her nipples.

"I wanna talk to you in silence," I said as I looked her in the eyes.

"How can we do that?" she asked.

"Let me kiss you, and my heart will say to your heart what my lips and words are too weak to express."

"I don't wanna fall in love. Tell me something to make me stop," Miriam said.

"Let me be the guardian of your heart."

"Never met a man who makes me feel so comfortable in my skin the way you do. I wanna bite you," she whispered in my ear.

"I'm all yours, my queen."

Miriam kissed my neck, bit me with fondness, and sucked my skin. She wanted to mark me with a hickey. A woman could leave love bites on any part of my body except on my neck. To access Miriam's cookie jar, I broke all my rules.

"Baby, if you give it to me, I'll give it to you. I know what you want, you know I got it," I sang as I looked into her eyes.

"Baby, if I give it to you, will you keep it a secret? You know I don't want no drama in my life," she replied by singing as well. "I'm so wet. I want you," Miriam whispered in my ear.

"I want you too, baby," I said as I tried to push her down on my bed.

"Hell no, maybe a hundred women have had sex on that mattress. I won't lie on it."

"I'll put a brand new sheet on for you, my love."

"Let's go somewhere else tomorrow," Miriam said.

"Okay, love, tomorrow."

Miriam kissed my lips and exited the room. As she bent down to put her shoes on, I glanced at her buttocks and craved to slap them. I sighed and shoved the thought away. I feared turning her off.

A few minutes after her departure, my phone rang, and I picked it up.

"Can I tell you a secret?" Miriam said in English when she got home.

"Tell me."

"I came commando to your house."

"What does that mean?"

"You don't know? Shame on you," Miriam said.

"I don't know everything."

"I came with no panties on to your house."

"No way," I said, and I giggled.

"You touched my boobs, and you saw I had no bra on. So I think you could have guessed I also had no panties on."

"Well, I'll pay more attention next time, Ms. Commando."

"Talk to you later."

"Later, boo."

Right after I hung up the phone, I put my hands on my face. I shook my head in disbelief and slapped myself for missing such an important occasion. I would have banged my head against the walls if she had changed her mind. I didn't want her to leave me hanging the way she had the first time she'd visited me, but I'd acted too cautiously.

I'm Scared

The next day, Miriam and I selected a hotel less than three miles away from where we lived. Public transportation stopped right in front of the hotel, but we didn't take the risk of going together. Once I arrived at the hotel, I booked the room, ordered drinks, and texted Miriam the room number. I'd called out sick from work that day.

While waiting for Miriam, I scanned the room that measured about four-hundred square feet. It contained one king-sized bed, a cozy outdoor type of table, a forty-two-inch TV placed on a high living room TV stand, and an air conditioner blasting air at sixty-three degrees Fahrenheit. The bed was covered with a pink comforter.

Two paintings that depicted the beauty of Haiti's landscape hung on the walls. One painting portrayed a Haitian market in the countryside next to a beach with donkeys carrying goods; women and kids buying, selling, or carrying goods on top of their heads; fishermen pulling out a fish trap loaded with fish from the sea; and different trees full of fruit. Just a reminder to anyone about what made the land a paradise. The second painting was an abstract with a personified sun and moon cuddling each other in the sky while a river flowing between them watered a green earth made with beautiful flowers. When humans live in harmony, love soaks their souls, and the earth stays healthy and displays peace and hope.

I put my backpack on a chair and then sat on the edge of the bed and leaned my back on the mattress. I inhaled the potpourri scent of the room and closed my eyes at the thought of penetrating Miriam's universe, extracting the purity of her soul, and discovering the warmth of her body. The thought bought excitement to my soul and happiness to my heart, even though I wasn't going to be the first man who'd opened her gate. "What if she doesn't show up?" I asked myself. I scratched my head and panicked. Miriam told me she'd stood up a couple of stalkers before. Although I didn't perceive myself to be a stalker, the thought gnawed at me.

"Where are you, angel?" I phoned Miriam to confirm.

"Are you afraid of a no-show?" she asked.

"No, just making sure all is right with you, my love," I lied.

"I'll be there in about fifteen minutes."

I stared at my watch and wished I could push the time to go faster. Damn it! Those fifteen minutes took forever. As soon as Miriam walked into the room, I welcomed her with a hug and kisses. I expected her to be happy, but she looked halfhearted and stood irresolute in the middle of the room with her hands clasped together. Miriam's facial expression raised my concern.

"What's the matter, honey?" I asked.

"I'm scared," Miriam replied.

"Talk to me, my love."

"Do you know Raul pays people to spy on me? He's wicked."

"We'll be okay, angel," I reassured her. I moved around, stood behind her, and then I took her in my embrace. I felt Miriam's heart pounding.

She became passive, not trying to hold my hands or to say a single word to me. Head down, Miriam stared at the floor as though asking it for wisdom or permission. I wished I had the power to navigate through her thoughts and discover her true intention.

As I wrapped her in my arms with my chin resting on top of her head, I stared at the beige wall in front of me, and I asked myself, "Should I cancel and reschedule for another day at a safer place or should I take the risk?" I panicked as well. I had never been in such a difficult situation. I also had another dilemma. Did I really love Miriam or was I simply seeking physical pleasure? I believed no one should undertake a life-threatening relationship just for physical pleasure in the absence of true love.

"Leito, do you love me?" Miriam asked.

Since my ex-girlfriend Sherley had left me in August 2005, I'd slept with more than twenty-five women. Indeed, I'd said to them, *"I love you,"* to convince them, but never meant it. I wished I could have been honest with those women and said, *"I like you"* instead. Those women sought love while I aimed to satisfy myself and feed my pride. Many deemed me a conqueror of women's hearts, when in reality, I was a coward—scared to give my heart to another woman.

I sighed, turned around, looked Miriam straight in the eyes and said, "I love you, angel."

"I love you too, Leito."

I kissed her lips, and then we sat on the bed. Blood flowed in my penis and I couldn't wait to penetrate her, but

I hid my rush and allowed her time to feel comfortable and relaxed.

Miriam took the remote control and turned the TV on. As she changed the channels, she kept saying, "Oh! Oh! Oh!" The TV broadcast only pornographic movies. She glanced at me and said, "Don't they think kids could be in this room?"

"Let me call the front desk to ask them to put on some cartoon channels for us," I joked.

"Oh, please," she replied.

We shared a good laugh, which killed our stress. Since I came with my laptop, a Dell Inspiron 9200, I took it out from my backpack and played some romantic Haitian Compa songs. I took her hands, raised her up, and danced with her. As we danced, we kissed each other's lips and undressed one another. The softness of her hands gave me goose bumps and accelerated my erection. Each time I kissed her neck, she quivered.

Full and perky breasts, flat belly, big butt, she looked like a glass Coke bottle. I questioned the purity of my hands before I touched the divine creature that stood in front of me. So I let my lips introduce me as I kissed her hair, her eyes, her lips, her neck, and then her breasts. I breathed in the aroma of the lemon blossom, bergamot, and jasmine of her perfume. Miriam-scented heaven.

Once I reached her fresh-shaved labia that had a peach fragrance, my mouth watered. I took all my time to roll my tongue on her clitoris and caress her breasts and her legs with slight touches from my fingertips. I watched her chest go up and down as she panted with her eyes closed. I inhaled the peach aroma of her labia and pressed my full soft lips against her clit and kissed it as though I were enjoying the best fruit ever made on earth. Miriam tingled and mumbled my name a couple of times, "Leito, don't stop... don't stop..." It was never my intention to stop because I planned to eat her up until she exploded before I penetrated her.

"Oh my God! Don't stop, don't stop... Don't stop," she mumbled in a fading-away voice until she quieted herself after she climaxed. Miriam leaned on the bed.

As she smiled in contemplation of her sensation of sheer ecstasy, I started a conversation with my torch as it pounded to the beat of my heart. *Put me in, Leito! Put me in!*

Mouth or vagina, which one you want to go in first? I asked it.

I don't give a shit! Get me in, man. I sighed, made up my mind, and pointed my penis at her face. Miriam gave me a surprise look that I could translate as, *I don't give blow jobs.* That would have been a complete disappointment for me. If I'd had one choice between sex and a blow job, I would have chosen the second option. I was obsessed with that.

Miriam grabbed my well-erected lollipop and licked it in a playful way. For an instant, she created a craving inside of my mind to lick my own dick and taste it. Miriam was having so much fun with my torch. She licked it and then moaned repeatedly. To me it was a penis, but Miriam made me perceive it as a delicious chocolate ice cream cone with the ice cream melting around the cone.

Enough, the pussy now, my torch snapped. I grabbed a condom and ripped the package with my front teeth. Miriam looked up at me and bit her bottom lips as I rolled the plastic down my penis. *I know you want it and I'mma give it to you, ma,* I said in my silent monologue.

I entered her universe. *Is this Niagara Falls?* my torch asked. Her vagina was soaking wet, warm, and soft. *Wow, pussy is wonderful. I think I will ask for an asylum and stay inside forever,* my torch added. I penetrated her in slow motion and watched her gasp. Miriam sighed when I reached her ceiling. She looked at me, and smiled before she closed her eyes. I kissed her lips and then increased the speed of the in and out of my phallus inside of her. Her moan resonated like a melody in my ears. We assumed many different positions.

A twinge of guilt wrapped me as Miriam was moaning and grinding on my phallus when I took her from behind. I replayed in my mind all the women who'd kissed me as if I were their fiancé, who held me tight like their precious and only son when I sucked their breasts, and who turned into freaks just to please me. I wondered what kind of magic or trick I used on them that made them unfaithful to their men and dream about having me.

The Bible says, "For all they that live by the sword shall perish by the sword." Did my actions set my fate? Or would the God of love judge me a victim since I'd been betrayed so many times in love by women who swore they would rather die than break up with me, or would he judge me as a heartbreaker?

While I sank into my deep thoughts, my penis became soft, and Miriam's moans decreased. I shoved away the thought of my standing in front of the God of love and being judged, to concentrate back on my assignment. Miriam and I had sex for about one hour. When we were done, we ordered food.

"Why did you pause so many times?" Miriam asked as she frowned.

"I didn't wanna come too early."

"Hmm… Why?"

I smirked and said, "I wish I could stay in forever. It's warm and the muscles inside your vagina kept grabbing my penis."

"Your penis fit me perfectly," she said as she took a sip of water.

"Custom made, especially for you."

Miriam grinned and shook her head. "You have a European body type. You're slim. You have long ears, big eyes, a pointy nose, flat belly, and good hair. You're so adorable."

"Thanks honey," I said as I kissed her sweet, soft lips.

While waiting for the food, I told her a few jokes. As we were laughing, someone banged at the door. For a few seconds, the thought of Raul catching us came rushing into our minds. Miriam looked at me. I stood up and tiptoed toward the door, my legs shaking a bit, and my heart pounding. The door had no peephole to allow me to see who was behind it. The person kicked the door again—*Bam, bam, bam*—and I held my breath. I gripped the lock of the door, inclined my head toward it, and asked, "Who's there?"

"Food is ready," a female voice answered.

I heard Miriam take a deep breath as a sign of relief. Yet I remained on my guard just in case. I opened the door a little before I rushed to help the waitress, who carried a tray with two big plates of food, and drinks in her hands. She shot a look at my penis, and then I realized I was naked.

"You should have somebody helping you carry the food," I said to the waitress.

"It's only me, and I'm used to it," the waitress replied as she tried to glance again.

"First time you see a cock? Do you want some of it?" Miriam snapped.

Ew! I frowned and then shook my head in disbelief at Miriam's comment. The waitress looked okay, but nothing about her turned me on.

Embarrassed, the waitress put her head down, walked inside the room, and set the food and drinks on the table.

"I thought you were gonna break that door," Miriam added.

"I'm sorry, Madame. I knocked a couple of times and I didn't hear anything. I thought you guys were sleeping," the waitress replied as she avoided eye contact with Miriam. The waitress must be stupid if she thought I'd brought that seductive woman here to sleep.

I'd ordered green plantains with fried goat for Miriam with a garden salad on the side and sweet plantains with boiled fish in a sauce for me. When we finished our meal, we sat on the bed and watched TV—porn. I thought Miriam had had enough and would ask me to go home. Instead, she slid closer to me and started caressing my chest and kissing my belly and then my torch. Miriam amazed me with her sensuality. We engaged in two further rounds of intercourse.

The front desk called the room and told us our time had reached its term, but we weren't done yet. Miriam and I laughed each time the front desk called the room and said they would charge us for another hour. We kept telling them we were getting dressed and about to leave the room. It took me another forty minutes to ejaculate from the time we received the first warning from the front desk. We then showered, dressed, and left the room.

When we got to the desk, the receptionist looked like a bomb ready to detonate. I paid for an extra hour and tipped her. Money brings happiness. She smiled brightly and told us to come back.

As soon as we left the hotel, we crossed the street. I was about to put Miriam in a cab to go home, and I would wait for the next one.

"You're not dropping me off at home?" Miriam asked.

Her question surprised me, but I said, "Of course, angel."

Miriam smiled, took my right hand and clasped it in hers. We took a minivan. We continued holding hands in the minivan. We found seats behind the driver, facing the other passengers. Everyone else in the car kept glancing at us. I freaked out and said to myself, *What if one of these passengers knows Raul?* While I was playing cautious and acting like a coward, Miriam somehow found the strength to remain calm and confident. She rested her head on my shoulder.

Once I got home, I sighed at the thought of being relieved of the stress of Raul's threats. I called Miriam and told her I needed to rest a bit, and I would call her when I woke up. She agreed with me. I took off all my clothes, threw myself on the bed, and fell asleep right away. I slept for over four hours. When I got up, I went to the dining room.

As I was eating, Junior came in. He jumped on me with so much pride as though he were the one who'd had sex with Miriam. "How was it, player?" Junior asked as he took two glass bottles of Cola Couronne, a Haitian soda with a tropical and artificial flavor, from the fridge, the best soft drink I ever tasted. He opened them and gave me one.

"It was okay. We had a good time."

"Don't hold back, tell me everything," he said as he gave me a chirpy handshake. Junior wanted more details— the entire story from the way I'd undressed Miriam to the moment I left her body shaking on the bed with weakened knees.

"Player, all I can say is… Mission accomplished," I replied with my mouth full of food. We laughed out loud, and I asked him about his progress in Judith's case.

I couldn't explain everything to Junior. I doubted he wouldn't become jealous if I told him about the softness of Miriam's hands, the melody of her moan, and the way her vagina gripped my penis.

Junior believed he was on my level and always wanted to compete with me. He loved to say to me, "Player, I know you're good, but I get laid way more than you."

As usual, I smiled and never answered him. I valued quality over quantity. I made sure I remained faithful to my mission statement—chasing smart and beautiful women inaccessible to all other men. After my meal, I phoned Miriam. It was already ten p.m.

She picked up on the first ring and said in English, "I thought you died."

I laughed. "Didn't you sleep?"

"Nope, twenty minutes after I got home, Raul came. He just left."

"Did he know anything?"

"I don't think so. He acted normal. He wanted to have sex with me, though, but I told him I had a headache," she said before she giggled.

"He didn't insist?"

"He did, but no wayyy. I had my jeans on. I couldn't have two dicks in one day. I'm not a hoe."

"Did you like the time we spent together?" I asked Miriam.

"Yes, it was amazing. By the way, why did you drink so much water?"

"I love water. It's my favorite drink."

I couldn't tell her the truth. Before my rendezvous with Miriam at the hotel, I'd drunk an eight-ounce bottle of an energy drink called Atomic. That drink carried its name with pride. It gave me endurance from out of nowhere. My glans became plastic. I could have gone for seven hours straight. The drink made me thirsty as if I were walking in a desert with a fire burning inside of me—a volcano. I sweated a lot. Even the air-conditioned room couldn't cool me off.

During a previous conversation with Miriam, she told me Raul never disappointed her in bed. I had to perform better than he. Raul beat me with the checks, but I couldn't let him beat me in the bed contest. I had prepared myself.

"What did you like the most?" I asked.

"Everything—nobody before you did it the way you did."

The word *nobody* made me frown. *How many men did you sleep with before besides Raul?* I wanted to asked her, but I restrained myself and said, "Be specific, my queen."

"You wanna know if you failed?"

"I want to better myself for the next time," I replied.

"Who told you there will be a next time?" Miriam asked.

"I was hoping."

"Your shaft is a little bit longer than I had expected."

"Call it Optimus Prime," I said.

"You're stupid."

We laughed out loud.

"To be honest with you, I love to be on top. However, you left me speechless when you took me from behind," Miriam said.

"You mean doggie style?"

"Yes, perv. I love the way you grabbed my hair, and slapped my cheek and then my butt as you were going in and out. I felt ravished and almost instantly orgasmed. It excited me and made me want you more and more. What about you? What did you like the most?"

"Your hands are made in heaven. They could melt a rock. Your moan kept me going. Now I understand why I nicknamed you 'angel'," I confessed.

"Thank you, Mr. Optimus Prime."

"You're welcome, Ms. Commando."

We stayed on the phone until midnight. Before she hung up, she admitted, "My day would have been perfect if I could have slept in your arms."

"One day, that dream will come true," I said before I wished her good night and kissed her through the phone.

The following night, we gathered on the porch for our regular meeting. As much as Miriam and I tried to hide our secret affair, our long stare at each other might reveal all. Through each gaze, we expressed our longing to be in that hotel room once again. Before I went home, Miriam grabbed my right hand, squeezed it, and hissed. "I wanna bite you," she said in English with gritted teeth.

"Let's go another session," I said.

"Okay. Next Wednesday, before I get my red light."

"Red light?" I asked.

"My period," Miriam said before she poked me playfully.

"Okey dokey."

Don't Get Involved

On a Saturday morning, I was awakened by a commotion in front of my house. I walked toward the window and took a look at the crowd. To my surprise, I saw a guy named Adler holding Linda by the hand. He said he caught her kissing another teenager around the same age. Linda, a sweet sixteen-year-old girl, lived with her parents right across from my house. I looked at everyone around them who stood like bystanders.

Adler grabbed Linda by the neck and jolted her forward and backward. I sprinted downstairs, ran outside, and pulled her away from him.

"Leito, it's not your business. Don't get involved," a neighbor said.

"She lives next to your house, and you all have the courage to stand and watch a stranger mistreat her like that."

"If she respected herself, she wouldn't be in this position," the neighbor replied.

I looked at my neighbor in disgust and wanted to punch him in the face for being a punk.

"If you have the guts, touch her one more time," I said to Adler, Linda's boyfriend.

"What you gonna do if I touch her?" Adler asked.

I stared at Adler in silence. My eyes widened and anger fueled my entire body— I was ready to teach him a lesson. I couldn't wait for him to lean forward and try to grab Linda one more time. I needed a good reason to validate my actions. I hated men who put their hands on women. I always said if someone cheated on you, violence wouldn't change a thing or make the person become a better one. Either you forgive or you move on.

Adler pulled his pants up on one side and pretended that he carried a gun. I rushed toward him, and people wrestled to stop me.

"You're trying to scare me," I said. "Because you work at the National Palace as a plumber, you brag about your connections and think you can intimidate me."

"Leito, relax," one of my neighbors said as he pushed me back to create a distance between Adler and me.

"So because you have a gun at your house, you think you're a tough guy," Adler said. "Leito, you're acting up. You know I can calm you down."

Adler's last sentence infuriated me. "I want Adler to calm me down," I said as I wrestled with my neighbor to get to Adler. I'd had enough of his trash talk. I wanted to fight him.

"Don't worry, Leito, I'll get you arrested for having illegal guns," Adler threatened.

Miriam and Raul walked outside, and shame enfolded me when my eyes met those of Miriam. She shook her head and walked right back inside her house. I'd disappointed her. I felt worse when other people said, "I never expected such an attitude from you, Leito," or "Oh, Leito, I don't believe it." They put the blame on me for trying to protect a young girl, and believed confronting Adler about his treatment of her was wrong.

My eyes red with anger, I went into my room, sat on my bed, and then started talking to the wall. I concluded that I had a good reason to confront Adler. If Miriam no longer wanted to talk to me, that would be okay—I'd already had her cookie twice.

All about Love

Adler went to Jean-Baptiste's house to complain. He knocked, and Jean-Baptiste opened the door. As Adler was explaining the incident to Jean-Baptiste, Margaret came out and asked Adler, "How old are you?"

"Twenty-nine, Ms. Jean-Baptiste."

"If I got it right, you're twenty-nine and she's sixteen, right?" Margaret said.

"It has nothing to do with age. It's all about love," Adler replied.

"Not only is what you're doing child molesting, you're raising your hand to her."

"I love her, and she's cheating on me."

"Thank God, I wasn't there. I would have broken your neck," Margaret said through gritted teeth.

"All women are the same, that's why you support her. Jean-Baptiste, you're a man. You can understand me better."

"Get the fuck out of my face," Jean-Baptiste said as he pushed Adler on the chest.

"What I said is right," Adler added.

"You're disrespecting my wife," Jean-Baptiste snapped and he motioned toward Adler to push him again. Jean-Baptiste would kill anyone who tried to mess with his wife.

Margaret extended her left arm to stop her husband from going after Adler. "Next time, I'll take care of you myself," she added.

Adler knew Margaret's father was the police commissioner, and having relations with a teen didn't work in his favor. He could get arrested if prosecuted. Adler left and murmured as he walked away.

I Have Your Back

In the afternoon, I stopped by Jean-Baptiste's house; he was scheduled to go back to Jérémie the following day. Margaret praised my efforts to stop Adler from harming Linda. "Don't hesitate to break his face next time. I have your back," she said to me.

Margaret was born of an Italian mother, a missionary who came to Haiti and had an affair with Patrick, Margaret's father, who became a well-known police commissioner. For some unknown reason, her mother left when Margaret was one year old and never came back. Some people said she was ashamed of the nationality of the man who had gotten her pregnant.

Margaret grew up with the love of her father. Round face, brown eyes, long dark-brown hair, with a five-foot, seven-inch tall frame, she was voluptuous—a Caucasian with an African woman's body. If she didn't open her mouth, no one would know that she was Haitian. She had freckles on her body. I called her sweet and spicy. She could be the sweetest person and have the worst attitude on earth—it all depended on the side one caught her on. Margaret used to play soccer despite her nearsighted vision, a sport that she would die for. She stopped playing after an injury. Like her mother, Margaret devoted herself to God.

Margaret met Jean-Baptiste during a soccer tournament in June 2003. They fell in love and married. Many men in the neighborhood approached her, but she turned them down. Since Margaret knew what her husband was capable of as a jealous man, even before he was a cop, she never said anything to Jean-Baptiste about being chased by other men.

"Adler said you have a gun. Maybe he meant the one you have between your legs," Jean-Baptiste mocked.

We laughed out loud, and I said nothing.

Jean-Baptiste always said in jokes what he had in mind about me. My conquests of women created some insecurity inside of him, especially when he knew how much his wife appreciated me. I pretended I didn't understand any of his jokes.

The following day, Miriam called me. "Will I see you tonight, Mike Tyson? I didn't see you last night. I hope you don't wanna fight me as well."

"I'm sorry. I, I, I misbehaved."

"You never judged me for my mistakes. Anyway, someone had to step up to stop that asshole," Miriam added.

In the evening, at our usual time, Junior and I joined Miriam and her family on her porch. Right after Mona walked inside the house, Maurice stopped by and said, "What's up, *Pred*?" as he gave me a handshake. "Hello, my beautiful neighbor," he greeted Miriam.

"Chillin," I replied to Maurice.

"Can I sit next to you, neighbor?" Maurice asked Miriam.

"Not tonight. We're having a private talk," she replied in a cold tone of voice.

"Tomorrow night, can I take you out to dinner?" Maurice asked.

"I never said I was hungry."

"I see you're not in a good mood. I'll talk to you another day," Maurice told her before he left as he tried to hide his embarrassment.

"I can't stand him. He's so arrogant," Miriam said before she glanced at me and asked, "Why do they call you *Pred*?"

"They say I'm a predator when it comes to women," I replied.

"I think they should call you vampire," Miriam said.

"A vampire?"

"Yes, you're a vampire. You come out only when the sun is down. You like to bite and transform people. With your boyish face and your smile, you look adorable and harmless. If only they knew the real you. Once you kiss a woman, she's done. It's like you've injected some kind of drug in her and made her addicted to you."

"Whenever I see you, I'm thirsty for your presence and affection," I said.

"I can tell by the way you look at me and smile as if I'm the prey. It amuses me to know that you're undressing me with your eyes all the time. You're contagious."

"Soon you'll need a cure."

"Who said I wanted to be cured?" Miriam replied with a smile before she playfully poked me.

One day, a neighbor called me a tiger. He told me tigers keep killing even though their bellies are full—something lions don't do. Women came and left. Since I never complained, everyone pictured me as the bad guy. What happened in Paris stays in Paris. The more a man complains and looks for sympathy, the weaker he sounds.

Take the hit, feel the pain inside, and smile on the outside. Life goes on.

Lucky me, things worked out well somehow. Before a girl left, I already had another one waiting impatiently at my door. I had one philosophy—always bring a woman more beautiful than the one who left. I intrigued many ladies, and my name became an obsession for them. Led by curiosity, numerous women volunteered themselves in a quest to discover me, just to realize the cost of their naivety at the end—I uncovered them.

You're My Best

On a Tuesday morning around nine-thirty, Raul decided not to go to work, but to visit Mona at the grocery store in Cote Plage instead. As soon as he parked his car and entered the grocery store, Mona asked, "Oh, what happened? Why aren't you at work today?"

"I'm not feeling well, Mommy Mona," Raul replied.

"Are you sick? Have a seat," Mona said as she grabbed the chair in front of her cash register and gave it to him. Raul appeared insipid and disoriented. "Do you want me to make some tea or soup for you?"

"No, it's not that. I've been stressed lately," Raul replied.

"This country is unbelievable. All countries are moving forward—Haiti is going backward," Mona said. She thought Raul was affected by the latest news of a traffic accident in Morne Tapion. The brake system of a bus that carried sixty-three passengers failed as the bus drove down the hill—leaving no survivors. That bus had failed the vehicle inspection a few days before, yet it was transporting passengers.

"It's not the country, it's Miriam," Raul replied.

"What did she do to you?"

"I want half-a-dozen of evaporated milk," a customer said.

"There's no more left," Mona replied.

"Mona, I'm looking at the milk right in front of me," the customer added.

"We're closed now. Come back later," Mona said as she shut the door to the grocery store.

"Poor people will always be poor. They don't know how to do business. You come to buy something, and they close the door in your face. Customers should be kings, but in this jungle, vendors are," the customer said and cussed out Mona while walking away. Deep inside, he knew he would come back because no other vendor matched Mona's prices. She made a profit on the volume sold instead of the price.

Raul's presence raised Mona's concern, especially since he had given her money to set up the business. Mona wanted to make sure everything went well between Raul and her daughter. She wanted to secure Miriam's future.

"Sorry, my son, talk to me," Mona said as she sat down on a bag of rice.

"Mommy Mona, you know how much I love Miriam and want the best for her. However, I won't have myself killed."

"I don't get it," Mona said in confusion as she raised her hands.

"Miriam is seeing that guy next door. They told me he has guns. You know this country. You see people but you don't know them. I can't risk my life and the future of my three kids."

"I agree with you," Mona said as she nodded.

"I won't come over anymore because I spoke to Miriam many times. She's being stubborn and said she won't stop seeing him."

"Miriam said that to you, and it's only now you're telling me this?" Mona asked.

"I thought she was wiser and would have understood me but…"

"Don't worry. I'll fix that. I consider you my son, and you know I don't tolerate certain things."

"I had a friend of mine. He died like this. He was helping a woman he loved, and the woman had a boyfriend. Next thing you know, he and the boyfriend had an altercation, and the boyfriend killed him. My dear friend left two kids behind. He was the head of the household. Now the kids are begging for food." Raul fabricated this story to tug at Mona's heart.

"I've heard stories like that before. Don't worry. I'll fix it."

Mona and Raul had a conversation for about two hours before he left and drove back to his house. Mona reopened the door of the grocery. She felt disturbed for the rest of the day. Judith brought her food, and she couldn't eat. Her worries had taken her appetite away. She liked Raul.

Mona closed the grocery store a bit earlier than the normal hours and went back home. As soon as she entered the house, she saw Miriam listening to music in the living room.

"You came home early today," Miriam said before she stood up and kissed her mom on the cheek.

"Miriam, what's going on with you lately?" Mona asked as she crossed her arms.

"I don't understand," Miriam replied with a confused look.

"You've been hanging out a lot with this kid."

"Which kid, Mom?"

"Don't pretend you don't know who I'm talking about. The kid who lives next door." Mona raised her voice.

"Oh! Leito. He's not a kid, Mom. I'm only two years older than him."

"So, you're babysitting now?"

"I don't see anything wrong with that. He's respectful. At least I have a friend."

"Anyway, he's here every night, and Raul isn't happy about that."

"Raul has his family. I need a friend, Mom," Miriam said.

"I understand, but this kid isn't the best choice."

"Again with this kid...his name is Leito. Why do you think he can't be my friend?"

"I'm not his mother, so I don't need to know his name. Don't you see your Leito has many ladies who come to his house every single day? You wanna join the line?"

"What are you talking about, Mom? None of his women are more beautiful than me."

"It seems like you already made up your mind. Anyway, I hope wisdom catches you before it's too late."

"Honestly, I don't love Raul. He's five feet, bald, chunky, and eighteen years older than me. Raul looks more like my father than my boyfriend." Miriam glared at her mother.

"Have you lost your mind? Now you met this kid, and Raul has all these problems." Mona really did want the best for her daughter, and she liked Raul's stability.

"The only thing I like about Raul is the fact he's always well dressed. His skin is way too dark. His nose, so big and flat, you can't even see his face. He's so possessive, I feel like a bird in a cage. I don't see him as the father of my child."

"Ingrate—you'd rather have a tall man who can't feed you?"

"I need my own man, Mom."

"I understand, but what can this kid do for you? Even though you decide to go crazy and act as if you're above the rules, an entire world is watching us. The boy is making less than nine-thousand Gourdes a month as a teller. The rent alone is seventy-five-thousand Gourdes a year. What are we going to eat? He has a brother and a sister who depend on him. Did you think about them? You're running straight to failure and misery."

"I don't work because Raul doesn't want me to," Miriam said.

"When your father died, I asked myself what I was going to do with you. I felt like the sky had fallen on me. I cried every night. You're my precious treasure, and I wanted you to have a decent life. Your father left me so much debt to pay that I hated him at first. Along the way, I realized all the debt was never his lack of responsibility. He did everything he could to provide you with the best. Your father considered you a real princess." Mona recalled the sadness of the time.

"I used all my savings for his funeral. He was such a courageous man, a wonderful father, and a lovely husband. I couldn't do a cheap funeral for the man of my heart. When Raul offered his help, at first I was reluctant because he was married. However, he did his best to provide you and me the comfort we had when your father was still alive—even better. You're not merchandise. I can't sell you to whoever I want. I only want the best for you. You deserve the best because you're my best," Mona said as tears fell down Miriam's cheeks.

Stay Away

I was studying finance on the roof of my house. In Haiti, a house made with a concrete rooftop represents a great asset. A concrete roof not only sets the family apart from the masses, it's used to dry clothes with the warmth of the sun, and as a place to study or observe the area.

As I focused on my book, a little rock flew by my eye. I looked over all the other rooftops around me to see where it had come from—I saw no one. So I walked to the edge at the front of the house, looked down, and saw Judith. She waved at me and asked me to come down.

I sprinted down with the hope of Judith carrying a good message from Miriam. They called her "Vivi" which means someone who smiles non-stop and shows her teeth. I used to be worried and afraid that one day she would say something to Mona or Raul about me and Miriam. Along the way, I realized Judith was not only a smiling and respectful servant, she loved and pledged her loyalty to Miriam. Sometimes Raul bribed Judith for information about Miriam's activities. Judith always stated she knew or saw nothing.

"What's up?" I asked as I pinched Judith's nose as usual.

"Mona wants to talk to you," she replied with a smile.

I had red basketball shorts on and white underclothes on top. I went inside my house and changed my outfit. Since Judith appeared happy, I thought Mona wanted me to help her with something. When I walked in, I saw Miriam sitting on the couch, her eyes filled with tears. She couldn't look at me.

"Have a seat," Mona said in a firm tone of voice. "I've seen you and Miriam being very friendly lately, and I would like it to stop."

"Did I do or say anything wrong?" I asked.

"Please don't embarrass yourself. I don't wanna put up a show with you. Stay away from my daughter."

"But..."

"Don't waste your words. This is my family, and I've decided what's best for us. I know you're a smart man and you'll respect our agreement. That's all. You can leave now."

Confused, I looked at Miriam, who didn't spare me a glance, and said, "I don't understand."

"Miriam has a fiancé. You know that already. I don't wanna deal with any problem whatsoever in my house. I want you to show some respect. You already have plenty of girls, and my daughter won't join that list. You can always say hi when you see us, if you want, but don't come here anymore."

Later on that night, I sat on the edge of my bed and called Miriam to hear her opinion of her mother's decision.

"What do you want me to do?" I asked.

"I love you, but I love my mother more," Miriam replied.

"Wow."

"I could always find another boyfriend, but I'll never have another mother."

"You said I'm unique and different, and yet, replaceable?"

"Let's be real. You're a lovely man, but it's not enough," Miriam replied.

"Baby, love is all."

"But all is not love," Miriam replied.

"What do you mean?"

"Leito, I have bills to pay, and you can't afford them. My rent alone is eight times your monthly payroll. What about food, clothes, and other expenses?" she explained as she raised her voice.

"Why are you talking to me with so much anger?" I asked.

"Please understand that it's not my intention to hurt you. I hold you in the highest regard, not because of the feelings I have for you, but simply for all of your accomplishments."

"You speak as if they're forcing you to do something you don't want to."

"I fully understand how you feel. I could explain more, but that would be too much. Maybe one day you'll be able to take me to the city of love that you promised me."

"Yup, good luck, Miriam," I said as my voice faded away. She'd crucified me with her speech.

"This is the first time you called me Miriam."

"It doesn't matter now. You just poured my reality into a cup and threw it in my face like cold water to wake me up. Bye." I hung up the phone before she could add even one more word. I tried to swallow my pride, but I couldn't. "Back at it again," I said to the wall as I released a puff of air. I turned off my phone and threw it on the carpet.

I felt dazed. I grabbed a bottle of wine and sat on the floor with my back against the bed. I drank the wine like water, just to realize that I had fallen in love once again.

Many praised my style and considered me one of the most macho men in town. However, they had no clue about my real situation. I always desired to live a simple life and fall in love with a beautiful woman with long hair who would respect and love me. I would treat her like a queen and honor her like my mother. I forgot one thing—beautiful women don't stick around too long with men who are broke. Not because they don't love, but because they receive offers from other men who already possess financial stability—and frequently women compete with other women for those men.

I had often been blessed to be in the company of beautiful women, but none of them stayed with me for longer than ten months. I couldn't take care of them financially. As handsome as I looked to women, my reality weighed poorly in the balance. My parents had died and left me no inheritance. The house I lived in belonged to my uncle. On top of that, my little brother and sister had put all their hope in me. I looked like a high risk—an encumbrance for the future of those women.

Their beauty represented their most eminent asset, and it had an expiration date in a country where jobs remained a luxury. In Haiti, they warned women to never exceed *Laj Almanak* (the calendar age—thirty-one years old*)* without getting married and building a family. That calendar age represented a challenge and a burden. It caused many women to make bad decisions.

Love Sickness

For two nights in a row, I walked by Miriam's porch and saw her sitting with her mother and Judith. I kept my eyes straight ahead without glancing at them or saying hello. I acted like a complete stranger. On the third night, before I went to sleep, Junior walked into my room and said, "Player, I have a message for you."

"What's up?" I replied.

"Miriam said she's not your enemy. You can always say hello when you see her."

I nodded, rolled over on my bed, and wrapped my body in the sheet. "Close the door when you leave," I said. Thank God, Junior knew me well, especially when I was feeling down emotionally. He added no words and removed himself from my bedroom.

The following nights, I managed to greet Miriam and her mother by waving at them. No words were exchanged between us. Those moments felt so awkward that I stopped walking by Miriam's porch at night.

Two weeks later in the middle of the night, a heavy rain that lasted about two hours became a turning point in my relationship with Miriam. We had a little bridge of about four feet wide in the neighborhood; it routinely got clogged with all types of debris. Water flooded all the houses within the vicinity, including Mona's—eleven homes in total. The muddy water reached about five feet high in those houses. Important documents were lost or damaged. Clothes, shoes, furniture, mattresses, all were soaked in that filthy water.

Fortunately for me, I lived on the second floor of my uncle's house. The first floor was vacant and available for rent. During a heavy rain such as this, the ground turned into a mini pool. The people affected by the flood spent that night on their feet.

Early the next morning, a few young men and I went under the bridge and cleared it a bit. We had to make small holes in the walls of three different houses, including Mona's, to get rid of the muddy water.

"Neighbor, I know you're cleaning, so I brought you something to eat," Maurice said to Miriam.

"Don't offer me a plate of food and ask me for sex later on," Miriam replied in a firm tone.

"Neighbor, I don't know what I did to you to make you hate me like that," Maurice said.

Miriam glared at him. He shrugged, walked away, and served food to other neighbors. Maurice had brought food for everyone. Miriam and I shared no words that day other than a "thank you" she said at the end.

We spent hours helping each other, and yet much work was still left undone. Like many other neighbors, Miriam had to throw away some home furnishings. Three days later, Mona and her family rented another house and moved to Cote Plage 26 with Raul. He was funding their move and made most of the decisions.

After Mona asked me to stop all communication with her daughter, and Miriam agreed to obey her mother, I convinced myself that I would find another woman or chase Rachelle. At first their decision didn't affect me too much. I had feelings for Miriam, but my intentions had been purely sexual. Although not being able to talk to Miriam anymore saddened me, I felt satisfied at the thought of having had access to her cookie jar a couple of times, and I was ready to move forward.

As the days went by, however, things got a bit complicated for me. I couldn't stop thinking of Miriam. I saw her almost every night in my dreams. Whenever I had a pen or pencil in my hand, I would write down her name. Whenever my phone rang, her name rose first in my mind as the caller. Her soft hands, her sweet moan, the scent of peach from her soaking-wet vagina, her smile, her humorous way of teasing me—all those memories started haunting me like a ghost. Her absence deprived me of sleep. The more I wrestled with myself to forget about Miriam, the more I desired to kiss her and hold her in my embrace. I missed her more each day. I was emotionally drained and slowly dying on the inside.

I never expected Miriam's departure would affect me that much. I called Emma and had sex with her that night to help me forget about Miriam. It didn't work. I tried with Nathalie and then Sofia—still nothing. None of the other women could fill the gap Miriam had left in me. I lost focus and interest in everything. I had no more energy left. Food tasted awful in my mouth. I went through a great depression. I comprehended I was in love with Miriam.

Jean-Baptiste and his wife, Margaret, visited me. They were concerned about my isolation. Junior and I were in the living room when they stopped by.

"We haven't seen you for days. What happened?" Margaret asked.

"Leito is sick," Junior said.

"Sick from what?" Margaret asked.

"Love sickness," Junior joked.

We all laughed out loud. I should say they all laughed out loud since I only showed my teeth through a fake smile.

"The hunter has his day and the prey has its day as well," Jean-Baptiste mocked.

"Leave him alone guys, this is not a joke. Don't make fun of him," Margaret said to her husband and Junior. "Leito, you need to do something about your health. You look sick and you've lost weight."

"You need to hit the gym man," Jean-Baptiste advised me.

"That's a good idea. I'll buy you some protein powder," Margaret said. She welcomed the idea with excitement.

Junior and Jean-Baptiste had a good time making fun of me. Not because they were bad friends, but we had a tradition of bullying each other. They made me laugh. Margaret comforted me with some words and told me that I would find another woman very soon to help me move on. Rachelle's name came back into my mind, and I felt Rachelle would be a great rebound. Margaret also told me she had a dream about me and that I would have a son by a Caucasian woman—a dream that made me laugh and hope.

The next day, I joined the same gym that Jean-Baptiste went to. As promised, Margaret bought me protein powder and some vitamins to boost my energy. Jean-Baptiste advised me to slow down on my sexual activities to gain strength and mass more quickly.

The gym turned out to be a great motivation for me. I went to the gym twice a day: in the morning from five to six before work, and in the evening from seven-thirty to nine-thirty. I became so committed and devoted that I even bought candles to light up the gym whenever we had a blackout. Aside from that emptiness inside of me, I looked good a few weeks later. Some ladies stated I looked attackable. I regained some of my confidence.

We Got Them

Two grey Suzuki Grand Vitara pulled out of the parking lot of the Toussaint Louverture Airport. Each car had two passengers in the backseat and a driver. The first car turned right and headed to Croix-des-Bouquet. The other one made a left turn toward Delmas. A quarter mile away, a motorcycle with two passengers bumped into the second Suzuki. The driver stopped in the middle of the street and got out of the car.

"You say a word and you're a dead man," Ali, the front rider on the bike said as he took aim at the driver with a Beretta 92FS.

"What's going on?" the driver asked.

Pow, Ronald hit him in the face with the back of his gun. "Shut the fuck up." Ronald jumped into the car, pointed a gun at the passengers, then covered their mouths with duct tape and tied up their hands. Ali took the wheel and fled with the car.

The driver stood up in the middle of the street by the bike, holding his painful mouth with his hands as blood started dripping between his fingers. A few drivers passed by and made a quick turn to avoid him. They probably had witnessed the kidnapping, yet they'd closed their eyes—not wanting to be involved.

A few people surrounded the driver and questioned him about the incident. He was dazed and bleeding profusely. Some pedestrians mistook the driver for the rider. Since the driver didn't provide any answers, they presumed the bike had crashed into the car, and the owner of the car got out, beat him up, and left.

"They kidnapped the girls," he mumbled after he spit the blood out of his mouth. The driver had lost two of his front teeth. He fainted and was taken to the nearest clinic.

Two days later, the captain called Ronald. "What happened to the job?"

"We got them," Ronald replied.

"Who? I dined with the family and the children last night," the captain said.

"What do you mean?" Ronald asked in confusion.

"You tell me."

"You said a grey Grand Vitara Suzuki, right?"

"Exactly... Wait a second let me pick up a phone call."

Officers reported to the captain the kidnapping of two students who had come for vacation.

"You have two women, one Haitian and one Canadian?" the captain asked.

"Correct," Ronald confirmed. is there a problem?" Ronald confirmed.

"Since when do we kidnap foreigners?" the captain asked.

"I didn't know I had to check their passport first," Ronald retorted. "The family said they'll pay."

"Don't pick up calls from them anymore. The embassy will track you."

"What should I do then?"

"Release them as soon as you can," the captain said before he hung up the phone.

"White people hold the country in hostage for centuries, and we can't kidnap one of them?" Pierre, Ronald's favorite disciple, asked with anger after Ronald had hung up from his conversation with the captain.

Ronald smashed the phone against the wall. "All this for nothing," he snapped. He sighed, lit a joint, and leaned back in his chair. He wished he could turn around and follow the first car instead.

As Ronald tried to figure out his next move before he released his captives, Pierre went upstairs and approached the Canadian woman who pleased his senses. He undressed her with lustful eyes. Pierre pictured himself gliding his hands underneath her navy-blue skirt, watching her breathing shallowly as he took her clothes off, and lying on her to feel the warmth of a Caucasian woman's body. His penis pounded to the beat of his heart. He couldn't resist his desire to have sex with her—to rape her.

The Canadian woman gasped when she looked at Pierre and saw his penis erect like a missile—aiming at her. As Pierre motioned toward her, she shook her head to implore him to change his mind. She called in vain upon all the gods for rescue. As he moved closer to the bed, she breathed more heavily.

Her Haitian friend widened her eyes with her heart beating out of her chest. Powerless, she stared at Pierre moving toward her best friend. The Haitian woman's heart almost stopped when Pierre let his pants drop on the floor and exposed his penis.

Pierre slid his left hand underneath the Canadian woman's skirt and removed her mesh lace-up thong. She fought with her legs to chase him away from her, but in vain.

Pierre hushed her and then said, "I won't do you any harm. I'mma treat you right, ma."

The Canadian woman shook her head to express her disagreement even though she didn't understand Pierre's speech. She wanted to scream for help, but the grey duct tape on her lips prevented her from doing so. Pierre took a cord and tied her legs to the bed.

A crazy thought came into his mind. Pierre removed the duct tape from her mouth and released her left hand before he put his penis on her lips. The Canadian woman seemed to like the idea. Pierre closed his eyes as she grabbed his phallus and put it in her mouth.

The following seconds took Pierre's breath away. She gripped his penis with her teeth and pressed hard on it. Pierre punched her in the face with all his strength a couple of times and tried to open her mouth with his hands—but her grip was stronger than his punches. Unable to resist the pain, Pierre screamed, and all the gang members sprinted into the room, including Ronald.

To their surprise, they saw Pierre on the floor all sweaty, shaking, and bleeding to death with half of his penis missing, and on the bed, the Canadian woman with a bloody face and a piece of phallus next to her.

"Bitch ate my dick," Pierre groaned in pain.

"Who the fuck told you to rape her?" Ali asked.

"Hold him," Ronald commanded his henchmen before he motioned toward Pierre. Pierre thought Ronald was going to take him to the hospital. Instead, Ronald pulled a knife out of his pocket, grabbed Pierre's testicles and cut them off, including the remaining penis.

They all watched Pierre bleed and die. The Canadian woman felt great satisfaction at the death of her rapist. She looked at Ronald and said, "Thank you."

Ronald looked at the remaining gang members and said, "Touch any woman and say goodbye to your nuts." As he left the room carrying Pierre's genital parts, he ordered Ali to put the duct tape back on the captive's lips.

The next morning, Ronald walked into the captives' room carrying two plates of food with fried green plantains, meat marinated in a sauce, and house salad on the side. Ali brought two cups of lemonade. Ronald ordered Ali to remove the duct tape from the women's lips and help them sit on the bed. Ronald gave a plate to Ali to feed the Haitian woman. Ronald grabbed a chair, sat in front of the Canadian woman, and then said in French, "Eat. I'm releasing you soon."

The Canadian woman was surprised to see how well Ronald articulated his words in French. Even though Ronald looked scary, she felt that besides kidnapping her he had treated her right. The Canadian woman took the plate and ate. "Thank you so much. The food was delicious," she said after satisfying her hunger. She hadn't eaten for two days.

Ronald remained quiet and added no words until Ali put the duct tape back on the women's lips. As Ronald edged away and was about to shut the door behind him, he turned around and said to the Canadian woman, "He couldn't control his nuts, I cut them off. You love meat, so I cooked them to feed you."

Both women glared at Ronald and then puked at the thought of eating a man's penis and testicles. A few seconds later, they looked agitated and out of breath. With their hands tied behind their backs and duct tape on their lips, they choked on their mouthful of vomit.

"Swallow or die," Ronald advised the ladies. "Get the van ready. We leave with them in one hour," he commanded Ali before he closed the door behind him.

As time went by, the ladies looked purple from lack of air in their lungs. Finally, they breathed heavily after swallowing the vomit.

One hour later, the men returned, placed a bag over both women's heads and put them in a van. They drove for about two hours and left the van on the side of the street, close to a city called St-Marc, a port city in central Haiti. Ronald called the captain and told him the location of the hostages.

A few hours later, the captain told his squad that he'd received an anonymous phone call with the probable location of the women. They went to St-Marc and rescued the two women. The captain was in charge of a special unit in the Haitian police with the mission of eradicating kidnapping within the country, a unit so successful that they'd gained the nickname of "The Antidote," since the population considered kidnapping a virus. That same night, the public information officer of the police department had an interview with the local news channels in which she praised the professionalism and integrity of the captain and his squad, The Antidote.

We Are Mormon Preachers

Two days later, around ten a.m., two Caucasian men with name tags, Smith and Johnson, wearing white shirts, black ties, and grey pants, walked into the Bone for Bone territory. Each man had a full backpack. They appeared to be Mormons. A kid stopped by them and said in broken English, "Hey, white men, give me money," as he did the Johnny Manziel's money sign. Smith pulled out his wallet and gave a ten-dollar US bill to the kid.

The kid shouted with joy, "White men gave me money." In less than five minutes, more than twenty other kids surrounded the missionaries. The men walked deeper into the slum and handed granola bars to the children. Smith was giving the granola bars, and Johnson was taking pictures with his camera.

A few minutes later, Ronald became aware of their presence. As Johnson was about to take a picture with a kid, Ronald and his gang showed up and surrounded the missionaries. Ronald pulled his automatic Colt 45 on them.

Smith and Johnson remained calm and put their hands up. "We're Mormon preachers. We bring the word of God to you," Smith said.

"Give us the bags," Ronald said.

Johnson glanced at Smith. Smith took an envelope out of his pocket and opened it in front of Ronald. The envelope had five-thousand US dollars in fifty-dollar bills in it. Ronald snatched the envelope and ordered the missionaries to leave his neighborhood ASAP. Johnson and Smith sighed and walked away.

Ronald opened the envelope and gave two-hundred dollars to each of his gang members and kept the remaining bills.

"Easy money. I wish they would come every day," one gang member said.

Ali stared at the missionaries edging away as he held their money in his hands. He felt something was missing. He didn't want to question Ronald's authority, but he was thinking about the best way to convince Ronald to check the bags of the missionaries. Ali said, "Grand chief, you ask for the bags and they gave you five-thousand dollars right away. That means they have something more important in the bags. Don't you think?"

"They were taking granola bars from their bags to give to the kids," Ronald replied.

"Exactly. That's what I'm telling you. They should have given you the bags."

"They were scared. Those Mormons are rich."

"I feel they have something more," Ali added.

Ronald reflected on Ali's comment. He glanced back and forth at Ali and in the direction the missionaries had taken. "Okay, let's get the bags. If it's granola bars, you give me four-hundred dollars."

"I'm not part of that bet. It's only Ali," one gang member said.

"Me, neither," another gang member added.

Ronald and his crew ran after the missionaries. Since they knew their neighborhood, they took shortcuts. As Smith and Johnson were about to hit the main road to take a taxi, Ronald crossed in front of them and pulled out his Colt 45, "I need the bags."

The missionaries appeared to be reluctant to give their bags away; Ali came from behind and hit Johnson in the forehead with the back of his gun. Blood poured out and started running down Johnson's face. Smith looked at the bloody face of his colleague, and a million thoughts must have run through his mind. Ronald's entire squad had guns aiming at the missionaries' head.

Smith apparently realized retaliating wouldn't be a good idea. Therefore, he surrendered, gave up his bag, and asked Johnson to do the same. The missionaries walked to the main road, took a cab, and left.

Followed by his crew, Ronald went back to the favela. As soon as they settled in, Ronald opened one of the bags and said to Ali, "Give me my money. I told you." The bag was full of granola bars.

But Ali still had an intuition that the bags carried something more than granola bars. He grabbed the bag Johnson had carried and turned it upside down. All the granola bars hit the floor, along with a 9mm automatic, fully loaded, and two other magazines filled with ammunition. Ronald and the rest of the squad looked stunned. Ali did the same with the second bag. He also found granola bars, two guns fully loaded and the pictures of Ronald, himself, and some of the other gang members inside a small yellow folder.

"I should have killed them motherfuckers. They were undercovers," Ronald said through gritted teeth.

"They left with the camera. We don't know what other photos they have now," another gang member said.

When Smith and Johnson reached their hotel room, they called the Canadian embassy to tell them that the mission had been compromised.

Around two-thirty a.m., all the dogs within the slum started barking.

"There's a *lougarou* in the area," a petrified wife whispered to her husband as she shook him to alert him to the supernatural being she was sure was out there. She had recently given birth to a child—her third. The first two had died before they'd reached the age of one year old.

The husband rolled over on the mat where they slept, walked in the dark, and grabbed a machete. "Hell no, we're not losing this child," he reassured his wife.

In poor and overpopulated neighborhoods, the thought of *lougarou*—witches—had terrorized families for decades. The *lougarou* were human beings, often old women, who transformed into domestic animals during the day or into ugly creatures with wings to fly in the middle of the night, especially between midnight and four a.m. They targeted newborns and young children to suck their blood and take away their lives through dark magic.

"Take that sour orange," his wife said to him right after she filled his left hand with salt. "Hit her with the sour orange and the salt, and she won't be able to fly anymore." The wife had done her research and was prepared.

As the husband felt something or someone was getting closer, he sprinted outside with a machete in his left hand and salt in his right hand. Pow, pow, pow, pow, the husband fell on the ground—dead with four bullets in his chest.

"Babylon, Babylon," a young man screamed out loud when he came out and witnessed that a cop had shot the man. Babylon meant presence of police.

Law enforcement officers invaded the slum. Apparently, they had collected important intelligence. They surrounded the perimeter of Ronald's house before they broke into it. Like fireworks on the 4th of July, gunshots resonated within the house. Bone for Bone members retaliated.

Ronald stepped out of his room wearing only shorts. As he fired at the law enforcement officers, bullets bounced on his chest and his head, and yet he remained standing.

A cop got very close to Ronald and shot him with a shotgun from twenty yards away. The power of the bullet propelled Ronald against a wall. "I killed Ronald," he screamed.

This joy lasted only a few seconds; Ronald stood up, put a bullet into that cop's head, and then ran away. Two other cops witnessed Ronald's quick resurrection. Scared to death, they fired at him anyway—in vain

That beautiful house of the Gillette Brothers turned into an army camp, smelling of burning carbon, dust, and metal—gun powder. Eight gangsters were killed, and the cops thought it was a flawless victory of justice. As they exited the slum, the real challenge waited for them— Ronald, Ali, and five others had set up a trap. Ronald and his followers each occupied a house and fired at the officers. Children and adults screamed at the sound of bullets flying from all directions.

"Officer down," a cop yelled as he rushed to provide cover for the wounded.

Afraid of causing too many casualties, the law enforcement officers withdrew from the slum. Before they exited, they lined up seventeen handcuffed young men on the ground —gangsters—and put a bullet into each of their heads. They called the raid Operation Zero Tolerance, which meant that no prisoner would be taken into custody. Two law enforcement officers joined the afterlife and four others were severely wounded.

Agony and despair engulfed the slum. Even the few rays of light at dawn that shined through the bullet holes couldn't bring hope to the people. That raid left behind a neighborhood wounded physically, financially, and emotionally.

Speechless, some people held their heads in their hands and stared at their shattered homes. Others sobbed next to the dead bodies of their family members and friends. Everyone wondered if they were still dreaming or living a nightmare.

A neighbor turned on his radio, and the whole neighborhood sang in chorus the song, *"Ede m' chante"* ("Help Me Sing") by Boukan Ginen, a Haitian roots band. As he replayed the song many times, tears flooded people's cheeks while they tried to bear the suffering. They hummed at the wrenching pain to regain strength. That song represented opium and a balm for their souls.

While the adults showed their resilience, some kids ran around, laughed, and collected bullet casings. The innocent smiles on the faces of the children reminded everyone there was still a glimmer of hope in the midst of extreme darkness.

Seventeen young men swimming in a pool of their own blood—dead—hovels and homes devastated by a tornado of bullets, and a baby quietly sucking his mother's breast as she remained unresponsive—a bullet having hit the back of her head as she tried to protect her child. These became the main images in the minds of citizens who later watched the news.

That event divided the population, who had divergent feelings. Some citizens rationalized that the victims deserved it while others saw the executions as a barbaric act by the police. All were aware that during the prior two weeks, criminals had opened the door to the afterlife for six civilians and eight cops.

Maybe Another Day

Although far away from his family, Jean-Baptiste's deployment represented a great opportunity for him to explore the beautiful city of Jérémie called the City of Poets, famous for its cake-bread called Komparèt, made out of coconut and ginger. Friends would get angry at anyone who went to Jérémie and didn't bring back one of those delicious Komparèt. Jérémie was located in the Grand'Anse of Haiti about one-hundred-and-twenty miles away from Port-au-Prince. In that agricultural-based city, inhabitants woke up to the melody of the birds. No need to mention organic, the peasants didn't use chemicals to produce fruits and food that tasted quite delicious—a quality of life that gave everyone the desire to live forever.

One day, Jean-Baptiste sat on a chair underneath a mango tree and was eating a special dish called Tonm-Tonm made of boiled and mashed breadfruit marinated in a sauce with crabs, smoked fish, and lobsters. A balmy breeze blew scents of blossoms carrying peace. Jean-Baptiste breathed in. Mother Nature took him in her embrace and kissed him with love and hope.

Jean-Baptiste closed his eyes and thought about his beautiful wife and children. He wished they were here with him to enjoy life at its finest—away from that overcrowded Port-au-Prince. As Jean-Baptiste fell deeper into his dream, his joy became bitter, and his throat muscles tightened up— he lost his appetite. The long hours on the phone couldn't substitute for the warmth of Margaret's body when he held her in his arms.

A brown dog without a tail walked by and stopped right in front of him. Jean-Baptiste glanced at the dog, put his plate on the ground, and then said, "Eat with me." Jean-Baptiste could have kicked the animal or have thrown some food on the ground. Instead, he fed the dog as though it belonged to him.

The next day, a peasant came to Jean-Baptiste and said, "You're a good person. Your parents raised you well."

With white frizzy hair, wrinkles on his face that looked like sea waves, and hunching over, the peasant appeared to be in his late eighties. His narrow face had the shape of an upside-down pyramid. His long, gray beard made him look like a goat—a face that no one would like to bump into on a dark street. The peasant carried an artisanal bag over his shoulder and leaned on a cane made in the shape of a snake. He wore brown pants, a red short-sleeve Guayabera shirt, and no shoes.

"Thank you, uncle," Jean-Baptiste replied.

In Haiti, it was a sign of respect when you went to rural places to call everyone older than you auntie or uncle, whether you know them or not. The use of one simple word, auntie or uncle, could keep you away from a lot of trouble.

"Where are you from?" the peasant asked.

"Port-au-Prince. My father was born in Cap-Haitian and my mother is from Léogane."

"They died?" the peasant asked.

"Yes, uncle," Jean-Baptiste confirmed.

"Hmm… you have a good angel protecting you."

Jean-Baptiste smiled and then said, "Thanks."

"Are you visiting friends?"

"No, I'm here for work. I'm a cop."

"Right… You don't know who am I, do you?" the peasant asked.

"Not really. I'm just getting to know people."

"Hmm… Do you remember you were eating, and a male brown dog without a tail stopped by you and you fed it?"

"Yes, yes, I remember." Jean-Baptiste nodded.

"I was the dog. I'm Akolo."

With his mouth wide open, Jean-Baptiste stared at the peasant in disbelief.

"Life is a mystery," Akolo said with a bright smile. He patted Jean-Baptiste's left shoulder three times and continued, "Never stop respecting every element in Mother Nature."

Akolo was the most respected and feared voodoo priest in Haiti, with powers beyond limit. Certain voodoo priests needed a specific time such as noon or midnight to transform into an animal or something else. Akolo could turn into anything he wanted to at any time—right in front of you. Believe it or not, certain magical tricks can be done only in Haiti. Some voodoo priests could resurrect a person they'd killed with dark magic within seven days. Akolo could do it even after months. They called him the Mighty Akolo.

To maintain his power, Akolo had to kill seven people every month. Therefore, he targeted those who came from other cities. He tested their hearts the way he had Jean-Baptiste's. Akolo was well known within the entire country and the invisible world. However, not everyone could afford his services. The requirement for his service was never about money, but human flesh and blood.

"Ask me any type of power you want, and I will grant it to you," Akolo said.

"Uncle, don't think I'm disrespectful. When I do something good, I don't expect anything in return," Jean-Baptiste replied.

"One day if you need me, ask for me and anyone will bring you to my house."

As Akolo was edging away, Jean-Baptiste thought about the offer. He ran after Akolo and said, "How can I kill a guy who's bulletproof?"

"Hmm…. Hmm… I can't answer you that," Akolo shook his head.

"But you said ask you anything and you'll give it to me."

Akolo stared at Jean-Baptiste for a few seconds and then said, "If you really want to know, meet me by the sea at six p.m. sharp… Alone."

Jean-Baptiste's heart pounded as he thought about the probable cost of an answer from Akolo. A sudden fear grabbed his entire body. He wanted to cancel his request. Better to be alive with no knowledge than be dead after knowing a few secrets.

As the clock was ticking, Jean-Baptiste became paranoid and started talking to himself. His wife called a couple of times, but he didn't pick up. He was so deep in his thoughts, he didn't hear the ring tone of his cell phone.

Margaret panicked and called her father to tell him that Jean-Baptiste hadn't answered her phone calls and text messages. Her father advised her to wait until that night to see if her husband would call her back. Stressed out, Margaret left work early. As soon as she arrived home, she turned on the inverter to charge her cell phone and waited impatiently for her husband's call.

At a quarter to six, Jean-Baptiste hit his chest three times with his right palm and called out, "I'm a man! I am a man! I'm a man!" He started his bike and headed toward the meeting point. As soon as he got to the spot, paranoia gripped him again. Any animal Jean-Baptiste saw coming toward him, he thought was Akolo.

A few minutes later, Akolo showed up and said, "Close your eyes. Take off all your clothes. Turn your back to the sea. Take seven steps backward with your left foot only. No matter what you hear or feel don't open your eyes or say a word. When you don't feel or hear anything, roll over on the sand toward the trees. When your body hits a tree, open your eyes, get dressed, and go back to the sea, and then dip your head in the water six times. Don't talk or say anything to anyone. Don't eat or drink anything tonight."

Jean-Baptiste sighed and did as commanded without hesitation or any second thought—he became fearless. Right after Jean-Baptiste's first step backward, Akolo started a mystical prayer.

After the seventh step, Jean-Baptiste heard a strong wind coming toward him, yet he remained calm. Like the eye of a tornado, the wind embraced his entire body, starting from the top to the bottom. A few seconds later, he felt snakes slithering up him.

A voice within the wind said, "First, you need to shoot the gun in the air in all four directions of the cardinal points—north, south, west, and east—in that respective order. Then you'll need to shoot his shadow two times and then only one shot to his chest. Do you hear me?"

Jean-Baptiste nodded.

The voice from the wind asked him the same question three times, "Do you hear me? Do you hear me? Do you hear me?"

Jean-Baptiste remained silent and nodded again and again. When the wind and the snakes left, Jean-Baptiste completed the second step that Akolo had given him. He lay on the ground and then rolled over to the trees. To prevent any mistake, he turned off his cell phone and slept by the beach.

Margaret had heard no news of Jean-Baptiste the entire day. Her calls went straight to his voicemail. She almost had a heart attack that night. Margaret's father came over to support her mentally. He ordered the entire Jérémie police department to stay awake until they found his son-in-law.

No officers took a break that night, including those who had worked during the day. They were worried about their colleague. This placed a lot of pressure on the shoulders of an entire police department. They searched for him at the morgue, hotels, and hospitals. They patrolled the entire city, and yet saw no sign of Jean-Baptiste. The cops speculated he had either been kidnapped or went back to Port-au-Prince and lost his cell phone on his way.

Free Like a Bird

The next morning, Jean-Baptiste went to the police station. All the cops asked him the same question, "Where have you been?" He told them he went to Les Cayes to see a friend and had forgotten his phone at his house. They called the police commissioner to inform him of Jean-Baptiste's return. Some cops speculated that Jean-Baptiste had spent the night with a woman.

Jean-Baptiste sat down at a desk in his office and turned on his cell phone. He stared at it and thought about how he would convince his wife and what valid reason he'd had to vanish for an entire night. He took a deep breath and dialed Margaret's phone number. As soon as she picked up, she said, "Thank you, Jean-Baptiste. Thank you."

"Babe, I'm really…"

"You hate me so much, you don't know how to take my life away," Margaret said before Jean-Baptiste could even finish his sentence.

"Listen, babe..."

"You're trying to give me a heart attack," Margaret continued.

"What are you talking about?"

"Everything is fine with you. I should be happy with anything you do... Right?"

"I'm sorry, babe. Let me explain what happened," Jean-Baptiste said.

"What happened?"

"Okay, baby, I was…"

"You were with your girlfriend Rose in Les Cayes. I know that."

"Oh, my God. I told you the last time I spoke to her was seven years ago and..." Jean-Baptiste pleaded.

"Yeah. Why did you go to Les Cayes then?" she yelled. "Do you know what I went through last night?"

"I know, love, but you have to ..."

"Thank God Leito spent the night with us. He was…"

"How do you have the courage to bring another man into my house when I'm not there?" Jean-Baptiste asked. He didn't let Margaret finish her sentence. Leito coming over and sleeping at his house was all that he had on his mind.

"Seriously?"

"You're acting like a bitch. I'm away for a few months, and a man is already sleeping in my house," Jean-Baptiste admonished.

"You called me a bitch, Jean-Baptiste, after all you've done to me and that I went through for you?"

"I didn't call you a bitch. I said you are acting like..." Before he even finished his sentence, she hung up on him. Margaret then threw her phone against the wall. It hit the ground in pieces. She cried and called her father from another phone.

Jean-Baptiste dialed his wife's phone number numerous times, but his calls went straight to voicemail. A few minutes later, Jean-Baptiste's phone rang. "Hello," he replied.

"Jean-Baptiste, Margaret said you called her a bitch," the police commissioner said.

"It's not..."

"I'm talking. When I'm done you'll say what you have to say."

"I'm listening, father-in-law," Jean-Baptiste said as he tried to soften his voice a bit.

"Since when do you call me father-in-law?" the police commissioner asked.

"Sorry."

"I've worked so hard to raise Margaret. Even now, I can't understand why she chose you as her husband. She married an unemployed man and works her ass off to take care of her family. You just started to work after five years of laziness. And if it wasn't for me, you would have still been unemployed. I offered everything to my daughter, and yet she chose to be with you. She accepted all the pain and suffering for you because she loves you. Since you made that lucky catch, you think you run the show and can be disrespectful to my family."

"I... I..." Jean-Baptiste stuttered.

"I'm not done yet. Don't you ever say such a thing to my daughter again. Don't ever do what you did last night again. Remember I can destroy you in the blink of an eye."

"Okay, I... I understand what you said. I'm sorry for last night. Let me explain what happened between Margaret and me," Jean-Baptiste said.

"I don't give a shit about what you wanna say. This conversation is over," the police commissioner said and then hung up.

Jean-Baptiste knew that the police commissioner hated him, and if it wasn't for Margaret, his relationship with the police commissioner's daughter would have been over long ago. He was aware of all the tribulations Margaret had undergone with her father. The police commissioner almost cancelled Margaret's wedding with Jean-Baptiste.

Jean-Baptiste called his cousin, Nahomi, and asked her to go to his house.

"Oh, Jean, why did you do that last night? We were scared to death," Nahomi said.

"Sorry, cuz, I'll explain it to you another day. But now, I need you to go to my house so I can speak with the kids and Margaret. I called her, and it went straight to voicemail. Maybe her phone is dead."

"Okay, no problem, cuz. Last night, the police commissioner, Leito, neighbor Denise, and I were at your house. We had a sleepless night because of Margaret worrying about you," Nahomi said.

"Since you were there last night, don't worry. You don't need to go anymore. I'll call Margaret later. Thanks, cuz," Jean-Baptiste said.

"Are you sure?" Nahomi asked.

"I'll call you later." After talking to Nahomi, Jean-Baptiste felt wrapped in shame.

Later on that afternoon, Margaret finally answered his phone call and told him to forget about her existence.

She also told Jean-Baptiste that she would buy another phone for her kids to speak with him.

That was a tough decision for Margaret. After dealing with her husband's absence, she now decided to stop all communication with him. She'd had enough of his insecurity. Margaret felt she didn't deserve such treatment from Jean-Baptiste, while she was a good mother and a respectful wife. Margaret believed there was no love without trust.

Jean-Baptiste had Nahomi buy flowers and gifts for his wife, but still he didn't make much progress. Jean-Baptiste tried to reach out to the police commissioner, but the police commissioner never picked up his calls. The silent treatment was one of the worst punishments ever inflicted on Jean-Baptiste. To make matters worse, the police commissioner ordered the police chief in Jérémie to schedule Jean-Baptiste to work every day. Hearing the voices of his kids was his only consolation.

One week later, Jean-Baptiste met Akolo again in the streets and asked, "What would have happened to me if I didn't do, or forgot to do, one of the things you told me?"

"You would have needed to bring me seven hearts within seven days or you would have died," Akolo replied.

"Seven hearts of animals?" Jean-Baptiste asked.

"The spirit I serve doesn't deal with animals, only humans."

"You should have told me this before."

"It doesn't work like that," Akolo said.

Jean-Baptiste looked stunned and couldn't believe that a little piece of information from the invisible world could have cost him his life. "So... What do I have to do now?"

"Nothing, you're free like a bird," Akolo said as he raised his hands in the air.

Jean-Baptiste took a deep breath at the thought of being released from an evil contract. "What if I went straight to a church after that?"

"It wouldn't make any difference. Only if God himself comes down and seals your soul," Akolo replied.

"Have you seen God before?" Jean-Baptiste asked.

"Do you wanna know?"

"Maybe another day."

As Akolo was edging away, he said, "I forgot to tell you, if you were afraid you would have died as well," before he laughed out loud, transformed into smoke, and vanished in the streets.

Let Me Finish

Jean-Baptiste traveled to Port-au-Prince to see his family. He bought gifts for his son and his daughter. He knew Margaret loved roses so he brought her a bouquet of forty-eight red roses. As soon as he opened the door, his children ran up to him and clang to his legs—they had missed him very much. Jean-Baptiste kissed them on the forehead before he walked toward Margaret, who sat on the couch in the living room; he kneeled before her, and then said, "Roses for my queen."

"Thank you." She took the bouquet and put it on the small living room table in front of her. "Please," she added as she put her left palm on Jean-Baptiste's chest and created a space between them when he tried to kiss her. "I accepted your flowers because the kids are here." *Bitches don't get flowers. This motherfucker thinks flowers are going to fix everything*, she no doubt had in mind, but she couldn't express herself with those words in from of her kids.

"Are you still mad at me?" Jean-Baptiste asked.

"Leila and Hervé, go to your room, Mommy needs to talk to Daddy right now. We'll finish the homework later. I love you."

"Love you too, Mom," they both replied as they jumped like kangaroos toward their room in excitement over opening their gifts.

"I wasn't thinking straight. The word just slipped through my mouth. Why are you torturing my heart?"

"I'm torturing your heart?" Margaret asked as her eyes widened. "Are you fucking kidding me? When I met you, you had nothing! I hurt my own father to be with you. I ignored all the advances from other men just to be with you because I love you. For five years, I've worked my ass off to provide for this family. I sacrificed everything; I have no friends left. I don't go anywhere besides work just to please you."

"But, babe…"

"Let me finish," Margaret snapped. "I gave you all of me and treated you like a king. When I got paid I gave you the money, and you decided what we should or shouldn't do. I never complained to you about anything. In return, you call me a bitch." Margaret sighed. "A bitch... Maybe that's who I am, but only for you."

Jean-Baptiste eyes quickly filled with tears. Yet he managed to drop none. Her words penetrated the deepest part of his heart. He knew that he would never find another loving and caring woman like Margaret; she was a gift from heaven.

"Please tell me what to do, and I'll do it," Jean-Baptiste said in an unsteady and guilty tone of voice as he remained on his knees in front of her.

"Do you know that Leito hasn't come over since that day?"

Jean-Baptiste extended his arms, took Margaret's hands and kissed them before he left the house. As he walked, Jean-Baptiste had one riddle to solve in his mind: why Margaret was ready to lose all contact with her father to be with him, and now she didn't want to move on without Leito.

Blame Yourself

Junior and I were sitting on the roof of the house when Jean-Baptiste came and extended his hand and greeted us. "You're planning on your next victim." He referred to any woman who dated me or Junior as a victim.

"What's up?" I said.

"That's how you greet a best friend?" Jean-Baptiste hissed.

"How can I be your best friend if you can't trust me?"

"You change women like clothes, and Margaret always talks about you. I see how truly happy she is when you're around her. I tell her jokes, but she never laughs like she does when you're there. I'm a man and I love you. What about a woman who's weak and sensitive by nature? How do you want me to feel or think when I'm so far away and being homesick?" Jean-Baptiste said with his hands open and showing his palms.

"Don't blame Leito, blame yourself," Junior said.

"What do you mean?" Jean-Baptiste asked.

"Nobody can joke with you, Jean-Baptiste. You take everything so seriously. You're constipated. You're a bomb ready to detonate at any time. Even your children who love you are scared of you. Honestly, I really don't know how Leito was able to remain friends with you all these years."

Jean-Baptiste acknowledged the truth behind Junior's comments. He explained himself as best he could. I told him it would be a better idea if we became regular friends—the type who only see and speak to each other on the streets—no home visits.

"You gotta help me, S.O.S.," Jean-Baptiste begged. "If you don't wanna do it for me, do it for her. You're the only friend Margaret has. You know I'll suffocate without her."

"What do you mean by suffocate?" Junior asked.

"She's my oxygen."

I remained quiet and avoided eye contact with Jean-Baptiste.

"Leito, I don't think you need to go that far with this. Don't wait until he commits suicide to help him. You know men from Cap-Haitian, how they are," Junior joked.

They said that men from Cap-Haitian were the best men a woman could have. However, their jealousy could go beyond limit, including killing themselves and the woman.

"I'll stop by later on," I said.

"She said if I don't come home with you, don't even bother to come," Jean-Baptiste said.

"You're doing nothing here," Junior told me. "Just go. Margaret misses you too."

Jean-Baptiste and I left and went to his house. Then as soon as I entered the house, Leila and Hervé ran up to me screaming, "Uncle Leito."

"I bring you your brother," Jean-Baptiste said to his wife, who hugged me and then kissed her husband. Jean-Baptiste retrieved his smile and peace. I played with the kids while Margaret and her husband went to their bedroom to make up. When they came back to the living room, we spoke about a couple of things that had nothing to do with the dispute.

"Thank you for coming back," Margaret said as I left the house before Jean-Baptiste hugged and thanked me.

Margaret and I had such a strong bond that she told me secrets she dared not tell her husband. She would drop by and show me underwear that she'd bought. If I didn't like them, Margaret would return them. I loved to play with the baby hair she had. Margaret loved me like a brother and at a level that sometimes confused me. Yet, I maintained my composure and respect. I avoided eye contact with her as much as I could to not fall into temptation.

Pumping Iron

Rachelle invited me to come to Jacmel, a city located in southeast Haiti, fifty-two miles from Port-au-Prince. I was reluctant to travel that far where I knew nobody. I'd heard stories of people who visited other cities and never came back. They were killed and transformed into animals to work on plantations by dark magic. True or fairy tale, those stories could freak out anyone.

Like many Haitians, I grew up in fear of my own culture—the voodoo, the religion that liberated my ancestors from slavery. When I compared the Christian rituals to those of voodoo, I would definitely choose Christianity, as I did. However, I wished I had a better understanding and knowledge of voodoo—its strengths and weaknesses. I would have felt prouder that I'd picked my faith in freedom and not because of fear.

When I called Jean-Baptiste to make him aware of my travel plans, he tried to convince me to stay home, telling me some scary stories. But my lust conquered my fear and pushed me into this adventure. I would be the first man who'd slept with two members of the 3D Team. I couldn't miss that opportunity! I left my house around ten-thirty a.m. on Saturday and used public transportation for a two-hour trip.

As the minivan zigzagged through the hills and valleys, I opened my window and let the natural, pure, fresh breeze caress my face. I admired the beautiful landscape that existed outside the capital. The countryside looked like a picture postcard—too magnificent to be true.

When I got out of the minivan at the bus station, I called Rachelle. I glanced around and didn't see anything special about Jacmel. The bus station itself was dirty. The passengers and merchants created such a commotion that I wondered if I got off at the wrong station. I became anxious when I glanced at my watch and saw that twenty minutes had passed since Rachelle told me she was going to be there in five minutes.

"Is this the station for Jacmel?" I asked one of the drivers.

"Yes, it is," he confirmed. "First time here?"

"Yeah."

"To get to the main city, you need to take a motorcycle. They don't let us enter the city with passengers anymore," the driver said.

I frowned at his explanation. *Who made that stupid decision?* I wanted to ask him, but I figured that the motorcyclists had to eat as well. "I'm good. A friend of mine will pick me up soon," I said before I walked toward the main road. Tired of waiting, I took a motorcycle and entered the city.

Once I got off the bike and paid the driver, I bumped into the artisanal riches of Jacmel—handcrafted arts of rare beauty everywhere. The colonial townhouses made of brick with wrought-iron balconies built in the nineteen century stood as a heritage, giving visitors a glimpse of the area's resplendent past. The city was so clean, with electricity running 24/7, and beautiful women, I wondered if I was still in Haiti, when I compared it to Port-au-Prince. I fell in love with Jacmel right away and thought it should have been the capital city of the country. My phone rang and I picked up.

"Where are you?" Rachelle asked.

"Oh! Hmm..." I mumbled as I tried to find a landmark to help Rachelle locate me. I was supposed to wait for her at the bus station. "I'm by the Five Friends Depot."

"Okay, I know where it is. I'll be there in three minutes."

"She better not come fifteen minutes later or I'll melt with the sun sitting right on top of my head," I said to myself as I wiped the sweat off my forehead with a handkerchief.

Beep! Beep! Rachelle honked at me. I crossed the street and got into her 1996 two-door, red Toyota Rav4. I kissed her lips and she drove away.

"You rock with those sunglasses," I complimented her.

"Thank you, my Leito."

While driving, we talked about my trip. Rachelle advised me to come again during the carnival in February where I would be mesmerized by the handcrafted colorful masks and costumes, the music, and the dances. She also told me that she had booked a hotel for my stay in Jacmel. When I offered to reimburse her, Rachelle stated that she'd invited me, and she would take care of me.

Rachelle parked in front of the hotel and got out of the car. I followed her and admired the sway of her hips in broad daylight. I always had a thing for tall women with nice legs like Rachelle. Gorgeous as usual, she wore green high-heel, peep-toe ankle strap sandals, white short khaki pants, and a short green blouse that exposed her flat belly and cute umbilical cord gap. It seemed she'd gained about five more pounds.

As soon as we entered the hotel room, Rachelle squatted in front of me, unzipped my pants, pulled out my phallus and inserted it in her mouth—no caress, no kisses. I'd desired to take a bath before I started, but Rachelle had no time for all those formalities. She wanted me, and all the prep conversation had gone on during our phone talks prior to my arrival. I took a deep breath and let go of all the sorrow in my heart as Rachelle brought me to another universe. Later, I didn't even recall what the room looked like.

"I haven't seen you for a few months, and it got bigger," Rachelle said.

"Are you sure about that?" I asked.

"The first time I put it in my mouth I measured it. So I know what I'm talking about." She continued to provide me with pleasure, and then asked. "What did you do?"

"Nothing. I just go to the gym now," I replied with a shrug.

"So you made it pump iron too?" Rachelle joked.

"I guess the protein made it bigger."

"Hmm... Hmm... Hmm," she moaned as she licked.

Rachelle enthralled me with her skills. I felt as though she were extracting my brain—I would even say my soul. I wondered if she wasn't reshaping my penis. With her lips, she tattooed her name in my mind. I felt an infatuation for Rachelle right away. She did it with such passion and class that if she had asked me to give her the world, I would have conquered it within a week for her. I didn't know about Elizabeth, but I think instead of the 3D Team, they should have named Elizabeth, Rachelle, and Miriam "Team Blowjob" with Rachelle as the lead.

"Put all of it in your mouth," I ordered.

Rachelle tried and choked. "I can't."

"Come on top of me," I said as I sat at the edge of the bed. Rachelle widened her eyes. "Take as much as you can. You're the one in charge." I took off her khaki shorts and black panties.

In between fear and excitement, Rachelle climbed on top of me and managed to go slowly up and down on my torch. I took off her blouse, caressed her back with my hands, and sucked her boobs, which looked like pears. Rachelle had skin so soft that it felt like a baby's bottom. She was thrilled by my gentle touch and kisses. When my brown eyes met her hazel eyes, she gave me a shy smile. I glanced at her clitoris and grinned.

"I know," she said with a smile after reading my thoughts. "Most of the time, I'm walking and my panties get me horny." Rachelle's clitoris was longer than that of the average woman I was used to being with. It looked like a second tongue that surrounded my penis.

As Rachelle became more comfortable, she closed her eyes and slow-wined on me. Through a mirror placed in front of the bed, I watched the sway of her hips and enjoyed her moans. As her feeling rose, Rachelle clung to my shoulders and squatted faster and lower. The sensation took all her fear away.

When I extended both arms and slapped her ass, she jerked. "Give it to me.... Give it to me," I said as I slapped her ass to stimulate her.

Rachelle sprinted before she shivered and then let out a sweet cry—she climaxed. She shocked me with a charming "I love you" whispered into my ears.

"Me too, baby," I replied. I couldn't say, "I love you too," because I hadn't yet reached that level of affinity to pronounce such a strong sentiment. I came for therapy not commitment. I was nursing a broken heart.

"My legs are tired," she said. Rachelle stood up and stretched her legs.

I positioned Rachelle for doggy style. I penetrated my fingers into her hair and grabbed it in a ponytail with my left hand, applied a little pressure on her waist with my right to mold her curvy body into a perfect shape. Her hair was so thick, I felt like I was riding a horse. It kept me going and I started slapping her butt.

"Slap me.... Yes, baby, harder, harder..." Rachelle ordered.

I slapped her with the back of my hand. Rachelle groaned as she rubbed her butt on my third slap. "You asked for it," I muttered as I moved her hand away and smacked her again in the same spot. She cried, and I spared her.

I put her on the edge of the bed, face up. I inserted my arms in between her dangling sexy legs to make a V shape with them and then grabbed her waist. I used my elbows to keep her legs opened and to prevent her from moving away. I penetrated her once more.

"Fuck me hard," Rachelle snapped.

I banged her the way Mike Tyson hit a punching bag—Rachelle screamed. I grabbed a pillow and gave it to her. She grasped it with her teeth, and still her moaning echoed within the room. She was panting when I leaned on her after my ejaculation. We stayed on the bed afterward as she caressed my chest and I played with her hair that I had become so obsessed with. I glanced at her derriere and caught sight of my fingerprints on both sides of her thighs.

"You're gifted," she stated. "You did everything perfectly. Your eyes didn't lie."

"You can read my eyes?" I asked with a smiley face.

"Indeed. They told me everything about you," she said in an affectionate tone.

I kissed her eyes and sank into a slumber.

Around two-forty-five p.m., Rachelle ordered food and papaya juice with banana and strawberries. We ate and then she took me to a waterfall called Bassin Bleu—Blue Basin—a natural treasure hidden inside the mountains. There was an abandoned house not far from the waterfall where visitors signed their names; I was surprised to see that my name was already listed on the walls. I thought I was the only Leito in the country.

Rachelle used a pair of my boxers as the bottom of her swimming suit. The marks of my fingers on her butt were too obvious. Rachelle jumped from the top of the hill into two of the three deep basins pouring crystal blue water into one another. Those jumps tempted me, but I had no clue about swimming—shame on me who grew up on an island. Rachelle gave me some swimming lessons as she put me on her back, but I was too scared to learn anything. I told her I liked my spectator seat and enjoyed the spectacle she offered with some other kids who lived in the area. The other tourists praised her diving skills. We had a good time together.

In the evening, Rachelle took me to a pier called Yakimo. We stopped by a lounge for a drink and danced to some troubadour songs played by the locals. We strolled from the lounge to the quay, holding each other's hands like lovers as the stars in the sky shone brightly on us. We sat at the edge of the pier and watched the waves kissing the rocks. We kissed each other countless times as if we were Thomas Edison trying to create the perfect kiss that would illuminate the universe with love.

This was one of the most romantic moments of my life. I spent the night at the hotel with Rachelle—a sleepless night. We made love all night long as if there was no tomorrow. I found great satisfaction in watching Rachelle limp to the bathroom. *You got served, baby,* I said to myself.

The next morning, a motorcycle taxi dropped me back at the bus station. Rachelle had to pick up a friend at the airport who came to visit her from Boston—her ex-lover from high school, she said. On my way home, I replayed in my mind the nice moment I'd had with Rachelle. I couldn't wait for another one. She had taken good care of me and removed some weight from my heavy, broken heart.

Player Forever

The following day, Rachelle called me at work and told me she'd gotten engaged to her boyfriend, the one from Boston. They'd had a long distance relationship, but she never thought he was serious. He proposed to her, and she said yes. That news hit me like a wrecking ball. I became emotional and spoke to her in anger as if she'd belonged to me and betrayed me with another lover.

Was I cursed, or did I just have bad luck? I wondered why both Miriam and Rachelle gave me a taste of heaven and dumped me right back onto the earth. Once I got home, I told Junior about Rachelle's engagement in a complaining fashion.

"Who cares? You weren't gonna marry her anyway. Thank God someone took the burden from you," Junior said before he went to the dining room.

For a moment I had gotten caught up with that amazing day I had with Rachelle. The news of her engagement depressed me. She wasn't the drug that I needed, but as a substitute, she decreased my sorrow.

Junior brought me a Cola Couronne, sat on the couch next to me, and said, "Holy shit! You banged that chick all day, and another man came in and proposed to her."

"*C'est la vie*," I said as I tried to hide my disappointment.

"I guess I'll stay a player forever. I don't want any daughter... Shit!"

I thought Junior would be happy about my conquest, but instead it raised fear inside of him. Junior joined the list of those men who're scared of making a commitment to a woman because of what they've done to other men. Their actions haunt them and paralyze their hearts with a level of insecurity far above normal. They trust no woman. If they have a daughter, they become paranoid. Instead of communicating with their wives, fiancés, girlfriends, or daughters about how slick men operate to sleep with women, they build a fortress with jealousy as walls—fragile walls.

"Where's Junior?" a girl asked my sister.

"He should be upstairs with Leito," my sister replied.

"Tell her I'm not here," Junior said to me as he sprinted to the bathroom.

"Hi, Leito, how are you?"

"I'm fine thanks and you, Patricia?"

"I'm looking for Junior," Patricia said.

"You should have seen him on your way here. He just left a few seconds ago."

Patricia sighed and shook her head. She explained to me how much she loved Junior and all the hope that he gave her. I comforted her and advised her to take a day to speak to Junior face to face about their relationship. Patricia looked disappointed.

As soon as Patricia left, Junior came back into the living room. "Player, she's in love and I moved on a long time ago," Junior said.

"You're still having sex with her, right?" I asked.

"Player, I can't resist. She gives me the cookie, I eat."

"I told you many times, if you don't have a plan for a woman, don't have sex with her more than twice. The more you have sex with a woman, the more she expects you to be committed to her. However, if you love her, bang her as much as you can. Live all your fantasies with her. Tomorrow isn't promised."

Patricia wasn't the only woman complaining about Junior's lack of loyalty. Junior struggled to understand women's emotions. To him, sex was just a game, a game without rules. I called him "Bang Bang Lucky Luke." He wanted to sleep with every woman in the neighborhood.

Later that night, Rachelle phoned me, I picked up on the fifth ring.

"Are you still upset with me?" she asked.

"No, not at all," I lied.

"I just want you to know that I really like you."

"Like?"

"I love my fiancée, but I like you very much."

I thought Rachelle called me to ask me if I wanted to continue the secret affair we'd started. I struggled to hold back a "fuck you" that my anger so badly wanted me to say to her. I felt disgusted. Fortunately, we were on the phone, and she couldn't see all the wrinkles gathered on my face.

"Listen, I want to be honest with you. You may not believe me, but it's my truth. You gave me butterflies the first night I saw you. I wanted so much to devour you."

"Devour?" I said in astonishment.

"Yes, that's what I felt. After that, you became a riddle to me, a mystery."

"Thanks," I said as I tried to let go of my anger and selfishness to understand Rachelle's feeling and thoughts.

"Miriam told me she had sex with you, and you know for me to do anything with you, that's a no-no. Nevertheless, I couldn't resist my desire for you. When she told me about you and her mother, I jumped on the occasion to make my dream come true. I wanted to discover the man behind that great smile."

"And?"

"You're far above regular men. Believe it or not, that day in the street, I don't know what took over my mind, but I just did it. Maybe you got some voodoo in you and cast a spell over me."

"I believe you. By the way, you're gifted as well." I wanted to say she was gifted at giving head, but I didn't want to sound stupid.

"Can I tell you something?" Rachelle asked.

"What?"

"I'm all wet just talking to you."

"So why don't we stay together?" I asked.

"Would you accept being number two?"

"I have no problem with that," I replied.

Being number two was the best position a gentleman could have. You're not on the map. You're listed as a best friend or cousin. Your only responsibilities will be saying gentle words, offering a shoulder to cry on, buying gifts whenever you can, and having sex—free from liabilities.

"He's sincere with me. I don't want to break his heart," Rachelle said.

"But you just said I'm different?"

"Indeed you are, but I have to let you go."

"Why?"

"I don't know how long I'll be with my fiancé. For now I love him more than you. I hope you'll understand and be able to forgive me. He's the first love of my life."

"I have nothing to forgive. You did what you had to do. At least I visited Jacmel and tasted your heaven. Hopefully, one day I'll get another chance."

"Never forget you have a special place in my heart," Rachelle said.

"I wish you luck in your new endeavor."

"Good night, and thank you, Leito."

"Good night, love. Sweet dreams."

I drank two glasses of wine. I realized that I should be grateful instead of complaining. After all, I had sex with two beautiful friends—a record I should hold with pride. I played no music that night before I slept. Rachelle and Miriam did more than just open their legs to me; they enlightened my mind on women.

Smiley Monkey

Miriam felt lonely and depressed without her best friends, Rachelle and Elizabeth, who were living miles away. Miriam lost interest in everything. Her face became pale, her cheekbones started showing, her round buttocks flattened, and her beautiful brown eyes looked sunken. Ashamed of her physical appearance, she turned her bedroom into a safe haven and barely stepped out of it.

Greatly concerned about her daughter's health, Mona called Raul to come over so they could discuss what was going on with Miriam. Even though he shared his thoughts about Miriam's health, Raul had other things on his mind. He was upset. Since he'd rented the new house for

Mona and her daughter in Cote Plage 26, Miriam had spent only one night with Raul, which lasted less than fifteen minutes. Raul always stated he kept his wallet open all the time for a woman so she should keep her cookie jar open as well.

As Mona was thinking about a good physician to take Miriam to, Raul took a different approach to the problem. "Judith, come… Take this," Raul said as he handed a twenty-five Gourdes bill to her. "Did you see Mimi and Leito doing any suspicious activities when we were in the other house?"

"Like what, Uncle Raul?" Judith asked with a smile.

"Like man and woman stuff…"

With one arm behind her back and turning her body left and right, Judith gave Raul a puzzled stare as though she was trying to figure out the meaning of his question.

"Monkey, you act like you don't understand, meanwhile you could be fucking all the boys in the neighborhood," Mona growled.

"No, auntie," Judith pleaded.

"Judith, why are you smiling? It's not a joke. It's very serious. Those guys can get Miriam in danger. You don't know what they're doing. They could be criminals and thieves."

"I didn't see anything, uncle," Judith answered with a smile.

"Give me the damn money. You're worthless. Go clean up the kitchen before I bang your head against the wall," Mona admonished. "Don't even waste your time with that smiley monkey. She always says she knows nothing. I wonder if she's aware of her own existence."

Judith smiled, walked out of the living room, and went to the kitchen. For a seventeen-year-old girl, Judith had handled the situation quite well. She remained silent. Mona had cussed her out. If Judith had spoken, Miriam would have shipped her back to the countryside—her worse nightmare. Judith had almost died two years before when she was with her parents in Cotes-de-Fer. When her skin became pale and she showed signs of fatigue all the time, Judith's parents brought her to a voodoo temple. They stated many hated their daughter for her beauty and wanted to kill her with dark magic. They spent all their money consulting voodoo priests and not even one doctor.

When Miriam visited her grandparents in Cotes-de-Fer, she saw Judith and fell in love with that beautiful, slim, fifteen-year-old teen with long and curly hair, white teeth, and an angelic smile. Judith's parents agreed to let their only daughter go with Miriam. They said it would be less painful for them if their beautiful daughter died out of their sight.

Miriam brought Judith to a clinic, and they diagnosed her with anemia. Many Haitians in the countryside attributed the sickness of their loved ones to evil spirits and reached out for help in voodoo temples instead of at a clinic or a hospital. Judith could have been among many of those people who died from ignorance.

Judith remembered those days when she lacked food and cried her eyes out as her bones ached. One goat and three chickens were her parents' whole fortune. With medication and a better diet, Judith regained her strength, and Miriam helped her discover a new world—school. Six months after coming to live with Miriam, Judith bought two cows for her father and sent money to her mother to sell kerosene—gifts from Miriam. Miriam loved Judith so much that she introduced her to everyone as her niece instead of her servant.

A few minutes later, the living room door opened, and Miriam walked in. She kissed her mother and motioned toward her room.

"Don't you see me here? How come you don't greet me?" Raul asked.

"You're spending a few bucks on us, but you don't own us," Miriam replied.

"Oh yeah...a few bucks... I pay for this house. I put food on the table, and I dress you. Whatever you need I give it to you." The words *few bucks* sounded disrespectful and hit Raul's pride like a ton of bricks.

"Anybody else could have done it for us," Miriam said.

"Now you think you're all this and that, but if it wasn't for me, you would've been dead already."

Mona intervened. "What do you mean if it wasn't for you, we would have been dead already? I remember you were the one who offered your help. We never begged for it. On top of that, you're fucking my only daughter. Did you think you were coming here for a free pussy fountain and could get as many refills as you wanted?" Mona retorted.

Mona's words shocked Raul; he'd never thought Mona would go so hard on him like that.

"Mommy Mona, you saw how Miriam was talking to me, right?"

"Yes I do, but that doesn't give you any right to claim us as your possessions."

"Sorry, Mommy Mona," Raul said as he rubbed the back of Mona's hand to soothe her.

"Miriam, you need to work something out with Raul," Mona said.

"Mom, I'm sorry, but he said without him we would die. So I'll show him that we can live without him."

"What are you gaining from this when you'll come back to me anyway?" Raul asked. His frustration from not having sex with Miriam made him choose the worst possible words. He aggravated Miriam.

"I can't breathe because of you. You're like a chain around my neck that strangles me," Miriam yelled. "I don't want you in my life anymore. I'm tired of being your side chick."

"So… all of a sudden you become jealous?" Raul said in sarcasm.

"You know what, let me leave because I have nothing else to discuss with you," Miriam said as she exited the house.

"Miriam, if you leave this house now, you're not coming back," Mona said.

"No worries, Mom. Put all my clothes in a bag for me, and I'll pick them up," Miriam replied before she slammed the door behind her and exited the house. This had worked out perfectly well for Miriam. She was looking for a reason to get rid of Raul, and she capitalized on his mistake.

Miriam's reaction left both Mona and Raul speechless. A few minutes later, Raul stood up and then said, "Call me when she comes to her senses. Miriam is old enough to choose what's good for her—or not." Raul went back to his family.

Raul's speech didn't even penetrate Mona's ears. She became scared and worried about her daughter. She wondered where Miriam had gone. Mona walked outside to pursue Miriam. "Sorry, neighbor, how are you? Did you see which way my daughter went by any chance?" Mona asked a couple of people on the street.

　　None of them could give her a precise direction. Some said they saw her going north, and others stated south. The confusion increased Mona's fear. She felt out of breath and went back home. The night passed. Miriam didn't come home, and Mona never closed her eyes.

Live My Life

At dawn, Miriam returned home. *Bam,* Mona greeted her with a slap on the face. "Where were you last night?" *Bam*, Mona administered a second slap to Miriam, who failed to answer her. "I'm waiting for an answer."

"Mom, you can beat me up as much as you like, but it won't change anything. I'm here to pick up my clothes and leave," Miriam answered as tears rolled down her face.

Bam, a third slap. "I'll kill you today," Mona said.

Miriam remained still as Mona threw a couple of punches to her face and body.

Judith stood in a corner shaking in fear and disbelief as she watched Miriam absorb the blows with zero retaliation. Judith couldn't prevent herself from crying as if she were the one receiving the punches. Judith loved Miriam.

"Better you kill me than someone else. At least I will be with my father who loved me more than anyone on this earth," Miriam said as she wept.

Miriam's last sentence hit her mother like an electric shock. It brought her back to her senses. Mona knew that her husband would have never tolerated a relationship between his daughter and a married man. Mona stopped, and Miriam walked into her room.

Miriam packed her clothes in a laundry bag and walked toward the exit.

"What will I do without you?" Judith asked in tears as she clung to Miriam.

Miriam rubbed Judith's back and failed to give her an answer.

"Why are you doing this?" Mona asked.

"I want to live my life, Mom."

"Why are you so much into that kid?"

"I love him, Mom," Miriam said as she continued to exit the living room.

"What about me? You're the only daughter I have."

"Now, you have Raul as your son."

As Miriam was about to open the door and leave, Mona ran up to her and pulled at the laundry bag. "Give me this."

Miriam glanced at her mother and released the bag. She was ready to go naked.

"Go see Leito. When you come back, we'll talk."

Miriam hugged her mother and said, "I love you, Mom."

"Go see him now before I change my mind."

As soon as Miriam left, Mona leaned against the wall and cried like a baby. She'd almost lost her only daughter. Judith grabbed the bag and put Miriam's clothes back where they belonged.

Miriam reached her intended destination—a hotel room. She took a nice shower and then lay down naked on the bed. Sank in deep thoughts, Miriam wished she had filled out an application to move to Canada with Elizabeth. Both Rachelle and Elizabeth told her that their lives had changed since they became financially independent. Although the long hours of work made them tired, emotionally they felt alive.

Miriam longed for that freedom. She realized that her love for her mom had impeded her progress. The majority of the decisions she made was to please her mother. The time had come for her to take charge of her life and live it as she'd always dreamed of. Miriam felt the urge to open her own bank account with money that she'd saved, and she started sending out her resume.

When Miriam came back hours later, Mona sat with her and shared words with her about life, men, and family. It was one of the rare occasions when she had a heart-to-heart with her daughter.

"You can always see the kid, but don't close the door right away on Raul," Mona advised her daughter. "Leito is a stallion. Before you let him jump into your pool, make sure that he loves you and he's the one you really want."

"Okay, Mom. Thank you," she replied with a wince. Her body was sore.

"Look what you made me do to you," Mona said. "Lie on the bed. I'll massage you." Mona felt sorry for her actions. Some old-school Haitian parents never apologized to their children. They thought it was a sign of weakness. "Judith! Bring me the bottle of Lwil Maskriti."

Lwil Maskriti is an organic castor oil made in Haiti. It served as a remedy to treat sickness, a beauty product to strengthen hair and help it grow, and it also had therapeutic benefits. Like Robitussin for some Americans, many Haitians believed Lwil Maskriti could cure any sickness. Mona rubbed the vegetable oil on her hands and then massaged her daughter's body. Miriam felt relieved and relaxed.

Spoiled Babies

Two days later, Miriam went to open a bank account where Margaret worked as a branch manager. She entered around lunchtime; customers were lined up and complaining about the slowness of the service from lack of tellers. Margaret invited Miriam into her office.

"Have a seat," Margaret said before she herself sat and then pulled out a flyer from a drawer. Margaret explained all the options available at the bank to the prospective customer, who later on chose the account that fit her best.

"You're so beautiful. How long have you been in Haiti?" Miriam asked.

"I was born here. My father is Haitian, but my mom was an Italian," Margaret replied.

"Wow. Every man must be chasing you in this office," Miriam said with a smile.

"You have no idea. They drive me nuts. Some customers come here almost every day and want to take me out on dates."

"I don't blame them," Miriam said as she filled out the papers. "Are you the only child in your family?"

"I have a brother on my father's side. He's studying in Spain now."

"We're spoiled babies. I'm the only child of my mother as well," Miriam said.

"You're as beautiful as me. You look Dominican."

"They say that to me all the time. Could you imagine if we worked here together?" Miriam added.

"You're too funny. I like to meet people with good energy like you."

As Margaret was double-checking the file, Miriam glanced around the desk and saw a picture of Margaret and Leito together.

"That's a nice picture you have here. Is that your... husband?"

"Nah, he's my brother. I mean, the type of brother I wish to have. He's my husband's best friend."

Margaret showed Miriam another picture. "Here's my husband."

"You guys look cute together," Miriam said.

"Thanks."

Miriam had heard Margaret's name, but had never gotten the chance to meet her. When Margaret showed her the picture of Jean-Baptiste, Miriam knew who she was, but pretended to know no one in any of the pictures.

"Your brother, he's kinda cute. Does he have a girlfriend or something?"

"Not anymore. Recently he was with a girl who lived not far from my house. Her name was Angel, something like that. She broke up with him. My husband said she was beautiful."

"Do you know why they broke up?" Miriam asked.

"Apparently her mother didn't want him for her, he said, if I recall everything right. For some reason, whenever he falls in love, he ends up heartbroken. He's a wonderful man with a great personality."

"How do you know if he really loved her?" Miriam asked.

"I have to be honest with you. Leito is a player, but since that girl left, many things have changed. It's like she stole his heart and all his passion."

"I would love to hear his voice or meet him one day," Miriam said.

"What am I doing now? I should be working, but instead I'm hooking people up," Margaret joked as she dialed Leito's number and put her phone on speaker.

"What's up Maggie?" Leito said after the third ring.

"Leito, I have a beautiful woman in my office right now. Do you wanna talk to her?"

"Sorry, Maggie, I'm not ready. I can't stop thinking about my angel," Leito replied.

"Okay, no problem. At least I tried," Margaret said.

"Thanks, talk to you later," Leito said before he hung up.

"He sounded sweet and heartbroken. He must really love that woman," Miriam said.

"I'll talk to him. I really like you and think you two would make a wonderful couple," Margaret replied.

"You have my number. Don't hesitate to give me a call."

"Did I help you with everything today?" Margaret asked.

"More than that. I'm looking forward to seeing you soon."

When Miriam reached home, she thought a lot about Leito. That phone call brought a number of memories to mind and created a craving in her to see him again.

Never Mind

On Sunday morning around ten, I went to a supermarket they'd opened a few weeks before at Diquini. Although another supermarket was closer to my house at Thor 71, I didn't go there because I wanted to walk a bit.

As soon as I finished paying for my groceries, I saw Margaret waving at me while she moved toward a cashier to pay.

"If I knew you were coming here, I would have told you to do the grocery shopping for me," she said with a smile.

"How would I be able to carry all those bags?"

"I would have given you my car."

I stared at her for a few seconds, and she understood the meaning of my silence. I was twenty-five years old and had no clue about driving a car.

"Never mind," Margaret said. "Wait for me and help me bring the bags to the car, and I'll give you a ride."

I chuckled and joked, "I'd rather walk than carry all these bags to the car."

"Stop playing around. I'm older than you. Respect that and wait for me."

I shook my head and moved over against the wall to wait for Margaret. She was the sweetest person I'd ever met, one of those special people whom someone couldn't say no to. Her soft voice carried such an undisputable innocence and sweetness, I wished she had a twin sister.

Margaret paid and pushed the cart full of bags toward me. I bent to grab a few bags as she held the door open for me. When I picked my head up, I saw the shadow of a man standing next to Margaret. With her left palm used as a stop sign, she warned me to stay inside. My heart pounded at the sight of a gun pointed at her ribs.

"You say a word and I'll blow your brain out. Walk with me toward this car," the man holding the gun said. Margaret did as commanded.

Nobody suspected anything aside from me, and I had been warned by Margaret. The man held her waist as though she were his woman. The more she edged away, the harder my heart pounded. Scared and confused, I stepped out and called out, "Margaret." She turned her head and remained mute.

The man turned around and said, "Maniac?"

And I called out, "Ronald."

Both Ronald and I were surprised to see each other. Ronald took his gun away from Margaret's ribs and tucked it under his shirt. He got into a white 2005 Nissan Patrol and left with another man, who sat behind the wheel.

Margaret stood speechless as she watched the Nissan Patrol driving away. At that precise moment some witnesses became aware of the kidnapping that was about to take place, but didn't happen. I sprinted toward Margaret and took her in my embrace. She was shaking.

As people surrounded Margaret to ask her what'd happened, the news spread inside the supermarket within seconds. The security guard sprinted toward Margaret. "Why didn't you call for help? Which way did they go?" he asked.

Margaret pointed north. The security guard ran in the street holding a shotgun with both hands to chase the bandits. He stopped in the middle of the street and fired twice in the air.

"What's going on?" a pedestrian asked.

"Two men tried to kidnap a woman in the parking lot," the security guard replied.

"Did they take her?" the pedestrian asked.

"No they didn't. They saw me coming, and they ran away. They're lucky. I would have killed them."

"It's always like that. You always would have done something, and yet nothing is being done," the pedestrian mocked.

The security guard walked back inside the supermarket as he managed to hide his embarrassment. Deep inside, I was sure he knew he would have never risked his life to confront the kidnappers. As a security guard, he worked seven days a week for more than fifty hours, and yet he only received a salary of less than three-hundred dollars US a month. As the head of his household, the security guard was the main breadwinner for his entire family, including his grandparents and cousins.

The manager of the supermarket called the closest police station and told them about the incident. The cops came within minutes. Margaret gave them the description of the car the bandits used and the direction in which they headed. The cops reached out to other police stations to alert them before they sprinted back through the streets in pursuit of the kidnappers. I knew it was a lost cause because they would never find the bandits, who were equipped with a better vehicle.

Right after the police left, one of the cashiers helped me bring the grocery bags to the car. Margaret and I got into her vehicle, and she drove back home. On our way back, I kept glancing at her, and she remained silent. I saw tears falling down her cheeks. Up until now, she'd only gone grocery shopping every other week with her husband when he returned to Port-au-Prince. Now, the first time ever she had gone grocery shopping without her husband, and she almost got kidnapped. I tried to comfort her by rubbing her right shoulder. I wanted to say something to her, but my mind was locked, and I became speechless. After parking the car, she said, "Leave the bags in the car. I'll take them out later."

I got out of the car, grabbed my bags, leaned against the front passenger door, and watched Margaret walk inside her house.

Olive Oil and Salt

Once Margaret walked into her house, she called her father and then her husband to explain to them what had happened.

"Jean, they almost kidnapped your baby doll," she said, weeping.

"What? Are you okay?" Jean-Baptiste asked.

"I can't breathe right now."

"What happened, love? You didn't drink any cold water after the incident?"

In Haiti, they always warn you to not drink cold water following a traumatic incident. The cold water could coagulate your blood, which will automatically lead to a heart attack.

"No, honey, I didn't," Margaret replied.

"Did you drink a spoonful of olive oil and salt?" Jean-Baptiste asked.

"No, daddy."

"Have someone do it for you, love," Jean-Baptiste said in a shaky voice.

"Babe, I can't talk much. I wish you were here to hold me in your arms."

"All right, love, I'll be there soon. Go drink one spoonful of olive oil with salt."

"I'm going to do it now," she said before she pressed the end-call button.

In less than forty minutes, the police commissioner showed up to see his daughter in emotional distress.

Maniac

As Ali drove, he kept shaking his head. He didn't understand what had taken place at the supermarket. He glanced at Ronald and then asked, "What happened? Why did you let her go and didn't kill that motherfucker who knows you?"

Ronald lit a joint. After a few puffs, he said, "On a holy Friday in 1992, I was on the rooftop of a house with my friends, flying kites, and having fun. I got so deep into it that I forgot where I stood. A few minutes later, I found myself screaming my lungs out, my right arm was dislocated, my left leg split in two, and I had two broken ribs."

"What the fuck!" Ali shouted. "Your parents didn't pay their dues to the *loas*?"

In Haiti, many people believed death, sickness, accidents of any type, failures, or any bad thing that happened had to do with the *loas*, the Haitian voodoo spirits—or was caused by sins, for those who believed in Jesus Christ. That superstitious mentality made the youth lazy and restrained their vision, and in some way held captive the development of the country itself. Nevertheless, when someone made a pact with the devil and didn't respect it, his family members died with no reasonable cause or due to an incurable disease.

"My father never set foot in a church, but my mom was a faithful servant of God," Ronald replied.

"What does this have to do with not kidnapping the woman and killing that motherfucker?"

"Maniac and I grew up in the same neighborhood before it became a jungle, and he was Claude's best friend. His mom took me to the hospital and paid all the bills. If it wasn't for his mother I would have been paralyzed."

"His name is Maniac?" Ali asked.

"No, his name is Leito. We called him Maniac because he was very skinny and not afraid of anyone. He was one of the worst kids to fight against," Ronald explained.

"What happened to Leito's mother?"

"Her death remains a mystery. They say she woke up and got dressed to go open her store as usual. As soon as she walked outside and went back inside her house, she died."

"That's strange. Was she sick or something?"

"As far as I knew, she was healthy. Many stories have been told about her death, but none of them stand out. Something went wrong, and nobody knows what."

"What was Leito doing with Jean-Baptiste's wife?" Ali asked.

"I have no clue. They must be friends."

"Fuck all that. The friend of our enemy is our enemy," Ali snapped.

Ronald looked at Ali and nodded. "I spared his life. His mother and I are even now. Next time I see Leito, he's a dead man."

A few seconds later, loud thunder echoed, and lightning struck a mango tree.

"Now I understand why you can't talk too much," Ali joked.

Ronald gave a wry smile to Ali to remind him that he didn't tolerate people making fun of him anymore. Ali wanted to make a last comment, but he dared not to because Ronald was on the edge of his last nerve. He could tell by the speed Ronald smoked the joint.

Part of It

Eight hours later, Jean-Baptiste showed up. Margaret was more than happy to see her husband. She jumped in his arms like a kid. He kissed her twice before he squeezed her in his arms. The police commissioner was still at the house. Jean-Baptiste walked toward him, shook his hand, and said, "How are you doing, Commissioner?"

"Okay, I guess."

Jean-Baptiste sat down on the sofa and his wife sat on his lap.

"Tell me what happened," Jean-Baptiste said.

After listening to the story from Margaret, Jean-Baptiste called me on his cell phone and requested my presence. Once I walked in, I shook everyone's hand and took a seat.

"Did you know the kidnappers?" Jean-Baptiste asked me.

"I know one of them," I replied.

"Which one?"

"Ronald," I said.

Jean-Baptiste and the police commissioner looked at me in disbelief.

"Do you know he's one of the most wanted criminals in the country?" Jean-Baptiste said.

"Yes I do."

"And?"

"And what?" I asked.

"You know him and never said anything to me. You were part of it," Jean-Baptiste said.

"Part of what?" I asked.

"You planned with them to kidnap my wife."

"What are you talking about?"

"I'm gonna arrest you and when we start whooping your ass, you will know what I'm talking about."

"Are you for real?" I asked him.

Jean-Baptiste pushed his wife to the other side of the sofa, walked toward me, and slapped me in my face. "Thief, I thought you were my friend, but you're a gang member."

I blinked my eyes as I tried to regain my composure. *Did Jean-Baptiste just slap me?* I asked myself. I couldn't believe what had happened. My best friend had slapped me and wanted to arrest me.

"Oh, Jean, have you lost your mind?" Margaret yelled.

"You're so naïve. He almost got you kidnapped," Jean-Baptiste replied before he grabbed me by my chest and said, "Put your hands behind your back. You'll sleep in jail tonight until you tell us about your gang association."

Jean-Baptiste pushed me against the wall, twisted my hands, and handcuffed me.

"You step outside with him, and you no longer have a wife," Margaret said.

"What do you mean?" Jean-Baptiste replied. "Are you blind?"

Margaret took off her rings, put them on the living room table, and then said, "You choose."

Jean-Baptiste released me and tried to grab Margaret's hands.

"Don't touch me, ingrate," she yelled.

Jean-Baptiste tried a second time to grab his wife's hand. He succeeded and then pulled her against him.

"You're hurting me," Margaret screamed.

"Really!" the police commissioner said.

For a moment, I thought the police commissioner had left the living room. He had remained quiet and observed all Jean-Baptiste's emotional actions. The police commissioner looked his son-in-law in the eyes and said, "That's how you treat my daughter?"

"Hmm…" Jean-Baptiste mumbled, and no explanation came out of his mouth. He released Margaret.

"Free the gentleman. If it wasn't for him, who knows where my daughter would have ended up today. I wish your brain was bigger than your muscles."

"So you think he's innocent?" Jean-Baptiste asked the police commissioner.

"I think you're sleeping somewhere else tonight," the police commissioner said.

"What?" Jean-Baptiste called out. "This is my house."

"I'll give you five minutes to disappear out of my sight before I change my mind and choose a place for you."

Jean-Baptiste wanted to break everything around him, but he knew the police commissioner wasn't a man to mess with. Ashamed, he couldn't look at his beloved wife. He walked out in confusion. Jean-Baptiste thought he came as a savior. However, he got kicked out of his own home like a villain.

"What about him? Who will remove his handcuffs?" the police commissioner asked Jean-Baptiste, who started backing away.

Jean-Baptiste came over and released me. Before he walked out the door, he stared at me with his eyes red with anger as if he wanted to tell me, *It's not over between us.* At that moment, I despised him.

"Thanks, Commissioner," I said before I left to go to my house.

My cheek swelled up following that slap. I could feel his fingerprint tattooed on my face. I didn't sleep at all that night. I thought of a million ways to get my revenge. All my thoughts led to one conclusion—I had to give a fatal blow to Jean-Baptiste.

The first and last time I got slapped, I was nine years old. My mother did it because I snitched on one of my best friends. A challenge fight took place, a friendly one between my friend Jonas and another teen named Wilner. This happened during the time of the karate movement in Haiti, and every little boy dreamed of becoming Bruce Lee. Jonas was living with his mom and sister. From a poor family, Wilner was considered a delinquent, a street fighter in the neighborhood.

I went to my house where Jonas' mother was visiting my mom. I told her about the fight between her son and Wilner. To me, the matter was a silly joke, but Jonas' mother took it to another level. She grabbed a belt and went after Jonas. She whipped him bad. Jonas came to my mother in tears. He said he couldn't believe that someone had the guts to say that to his mother.

My mother told Jonas I was the snitch. Jonas swore on his life I would never do that to him. His statement reached the deepest part of my mom's soul; she grabbed me by the chest, and hit my lips with the palm of her hands a couple of times. Each time she hit me, she said, "Keep your mouth shut."

My lips had some bruises, and after that my friendship with Jonas changed. Jonas approached me many times to tell me that he forgave me, and he'd like to move on. I refused because I felt I didn't deserve his friendship. That shame of betrayal would follow me to my grave. I promised myself to keep my mouth shut and not even think about becoming a news reporter, which had been my idea at the time.

Don't Lose It

Five days passed, and yet I still wrestled with my thoughts, trying to get myself together. I had a tough time sleeping, eating, or focusing on anything since the incident with Jean-Baptiste, my so-called best friend. My brain became the sanctuary of dark contemplation. I kept thinking about revenge, the only way to unleash my anger.

I mentioned nothing to no one, even Junior. That Friday night in my room, I drew up a smart plan to strike Jean-Baptiste and make him pay for his insolence. *There's an area of unfinished houses that Jean-Baptiste uses as a shortcut on his way to the gym. He starts his run around five a.m., and I'll be hiding in one of those unfinished homes waiting for him. And then... Bam! I'd have my revenge, and nobody will even suspect me.*

As planned, I left my house around four-forty-five a.m. on Saturday, and set myself up in ambush. A few minutes later, I heard footsteps coming my way. *That must be Jean-Baptiste.* I took a deep breath and let anger flow inside my veins until it invaded my heart and turned it dark. A bird flew and landed on top of the wall in front of me. "Tweet, tweet," the bird said. I was no expert at recognizing different types of birds, so I didn't know what kind of bird it was. "Tweet, tweet," the bird said again.

Where the hell did the bird come from? Does Jean-Baptiste have a voodoo spirit that protects him? The man never showed any interest in magic in front of me, but who knows? I ducked behind the wall—ready to strike. *What if Jean-Baptiste strikes me first? He's a cop and has better training than me.* I didn't flinch for a second—too late to back down.

The sound of his footsteps got closer, and I looked up at the bird for a last time before I acted. The bird glared at me in silence as if asking me, "What happened to forgiveness? What about your friendship with Margaret? How will you look at his children who love you so much and call you uncle?"

By the time I answered my own questions, Jean-Baptiste had passed by me. The clock was ticking while I stood and watched his back as he edged away without turning around—he was still on my radar. "Tweet, tweet." There went the bird again. Once Jean-Baptiste disappeared from my sight, the bird flew into the sky, and I returned home.

I jumped on my bed with my thoughts divided. My heart was trying to convince me to forgive, while my mind fumed that I'd failed to act and earn my own respect. Then a deep slumber stole over my body until the ringing of my phone woke me up. I struggled to open my eyes as I reached for the ringing phone. I felt as though my brain had shut down. The phone kept on ringing inside my room, and I couldn't pinpoint its position. Finally, I spotted the phone inside of one of my sneakers.

"Hello," I answered in a grumpy voice.

"Do you wanna work?" Miriam asked.

"Yes I do," I replied as I cleared my voice to make it sound smooth.

"Come to my house now."

I rolled over on my bed before I rushed to the bathroom to take a quick bath. Miriam's voice fueled my body with energy. I wondered what job opportunity she'd found for me through her network. I even started thinking about being paid in US. dollars. I pictured myself jumping on her to show how much I loved the fact she found me another job.

As much as I loved the bank and loved serving its customers, my supervisor, Gary, aggravated the hell out of me. He liked me so much, he had told me that I would get a promotion in three months. The customers praised my quickness and so did the managers because I made fewer mistakes than many other tellers.

I yearned to leave the bank. Gary was gay. I never considered myself a homophobe, yet I couldn't stand that Gary always whispered in my ear whenever he needed to tell me something or squeezed my shoulder when he stood next to me while I was trying to help customers. I hated that I often had to call him to come and grant me clearance for transactions above my limit. One day, he even slapped my butt in the hallway.

Sexual harassment belonged only in the dictionary in some places. Either you stayed or you got fired. Gary got on my nerves so bad that I wanted to punch him in the face. The bank had cameras all over except the bathrooms, and I never pictured myself in the toilets with Gary. If I punched him, the bank would fire me because I threw the first punch. Gary was one of the best branch supervisors the bank ever had, a punctual and honest man.

Part of the problem was that my co-workers took great pleasure in bullying me. If I had received the promotion Gary promised, they would have become jealous and accused me of sleeping with Gary for the promotion.

They would have ignored all the facts about my competence and hard work.

As I opened the door at Miriam's, I saw Judith sitting in the living room. She didn't even wait for me to say anything. "Mimi is in her room," Judith said as she pointed with her index finger toward Miriam's bedroom. I pinched her nose as usual and walked to the room.

I opened the door and I smiled. Miriam lay on her left side on her bed naked as though she were posing as a model. I couldn't believe it. *She better not ask me to draw her picture. I'm no fucking Jack from* Titanic.

"Close the door and come closer," Miriam said in a seductive voice.

I obeyed her, and my penis steered. As I got close enough to touch her body, she said, "Fan me. I'm hot." She gave me a pillow. As I was fanning her, Miriam gazed at me and undressed me with her eyes. "Did you miss me?"

"It feels like an eternity," I replied before I swallowed my saliva. I craved to penetrate her universe after those six months. Yeah! Six months had passed since Miriam moved out of my neighborhood.

"Show me," she said before positioning herself in the middle of the bed.

I dropped the pillow on the floor and climbed onto the bed. I kissed her hair, her forehead, and then her eyes. My lips met hers on the street of tenderness as I gently squeezed the flesh of her body, Miriam gasped. I continued my kissing journey by making a stop around her neck, then her boobs until I reached her clitoris. She quivered.

The following minute, an inexplicable thirst seized me, and I started to bite her. The feeling was so strong, I wanted to devour her—taste her blood and flesh. The stronger I bit her, the louder she moaned. For her, my actions were bittersweet. I bit her peach fragrance labia and then let my tongue caress her clitoris and rolled her hard nipples with my fingers. She choked me with her legs as she was about to reach her climax.

I patted her legs so she could release me. I needed air; I couldn't breathe. Unfortunately, Miriam was in a different world. I decided to stay calm and hoped she released that energy as quickly as possible.

Miriam shivered and then released my head. I kissed her lips and stood up to catch my breath. Miriam found my reaction odd and asked me, "What's wrong?"

"You almost killed me," I said as I gasped for air.

Miriam sprang from the bed and started to kiss me and said, "Babe, I'm sorry. You took me to another universe. I'm sorry." She continued to press her lips against mine and then pulled my black t-shirt over my head. She kissed my chest and sucked and pinched with her teeth my almost non-existent nipples. It felt so good.

I removed the remainder of my clothing, and before I could finish, Miriam was down on bended knees. She inserted my erect penis in her mouth. "I missed you, Optimus Prime."

"Optimus Prime missed you more than you can even imagine," I replied.

Miriam glanced up at me with a romantic smile and continued to amaze me with her lips and tongue. *There you go; she's licking that chocolate ice cream cone again.* My heart pumped more blood into my penis as I was mesmerized by the curvy shape of Miriam's buttocks when she squatted in front of me. *Oh Lord!*

Miriam knelt and kissed my toes with affection. That kiss went straight to my heart. She unsealed and conquered it. This was the first time a woman ever kissed my toes. I felt like a king. I gently laid her down on the bed and then I entered her soft, warm, wet universe. *Can Gary tell me that he gets more pleasure with a man than a woman?* Too bad for him—I would never trade such pleasure with a woman for any man. I thrust my phallus inside of her and went in like there was no tomorrow.

"Are you trying to dig your way to China?" Miriam joked a few minutes later. "I'm yours, yours only. Take your time. Let's enjoy the moment."

I smiled and slowed down a bit as the words *I'm yours, yours only* penetrated my mind and made their way through to my heart. "I missed you so much, angel. I wish I could enter my entire body inside of you," I confessed. I didn't realize I was so rough, until she mentioned it.

"I have longed to feel you inside of me," Miriam whispered.

I lifted up her right leg and held it against my chest with my left arm. I rolled the tip of my tongue on the sole of her foot, and she started quivering on the bed. I caressed her body and then rolled her nipples, Miriam shivered more. She tried to pull her leg away from my chest, but I held it firmly. I admired her body movement as I went in and out of her wet labia, her Niagara Falls. Miriam moaned and gripped her hair before she screamed, "Leito, Leito, Leito," and then exploded.

After we finished, I lay down on the bed, and Miriam rested her chin on my chest. She confessed, "I made two mistakes, asking you to look me in the eyes and kissing your soft lips. Cursed be that day my lips kissed yours, and they left me wanting more. I opened my legs to you, and you stole my heart and made me addicted to you." Miriam sounded poetic.

"I love you, angel." I meant it that day. My declaration came from the bottom of my heart.

"I spent a great deal of time thinking about you," she said. "I've spent my time crying over you the past few weeks. I love the sense of peace when I'm with you. I'm satisfied just being in a room dancing with you. I'm truly happy when I'm with you. I've never been in love before. I don't know if it's a wise decision, but I want to trust you with my heart. If one day I'm disappointed that our love didn't survive, I'll move on with the idea that I had a good reason to fall in love."

Her confession melted my heart. I became human once again. "I want to be yours. I give you the key of my heart. Be my queen," I said before I wrapped her in my arms and squeezed her body against mine.

"Good afternoon, Uncle Raul," Judith called out. She was trying to warn us about Raul's presence in the house.

"Where's Miriam?" Raul asked.

"She's in her room sleeping. She's had a migraine all day long," Judith replied.

I almost had a heart attack when I heard Raul rattle the door handle. I didn't remember if I'd locked it or not.

"Mimi told me not to let anybody in her room. She wants to sleep a little bit," Judith said as Raul turned the door handle clockwise.

Miriam remained cool and relaxed, lying on her back with her hands beneath her head. She didn't even bother to drape herself with the sheet. She wanted Raul to see us. Petrified, I froze on the bed as I tried to figure out the explanation for my naked presence in Miriam's bed—if given time to clarify.

"Okay. Tell her I'll come back tonight when she's awake," Raul said and let go of the door handle.

"Yes, Uncle Raul," Judith said with no sign of panic.

"Give her this envelope. That's the rent money. Don't lose it," Raul said as he walked away.

"No, no, I won't."

I sprinted to check on the door—it was unlocked. Raul often carried his gun. My life flashed in front of me. I pictured my photo on the front page of the newspaper: a stupid young man caught sleeping with a woman, who got killed by her man in her bed with a couple of bullets in the chest. I imagined my family rushing to bury me—a disgrace and a fool—and all those so-called prophets who would have claimed they saw that coming. People would have considered me an imbecile for making love to the woman at the man's house instead of going to a hotel. My life would have turned into an example and a joke told by generation after generation.

"Were you scared?" Miriam asked.

"Nooooo, why should I be?" I lied.

I lay down next to Miriam and caressed her body. I stayed at some distance from her because I didn't want her to hear my heart hammering. Judith had saved my life, and I would be forever grateful to her. I got dressed and spent a couple of minutes with Miriam in the living room before I went home.

I told Junior about my day. He said that was bad luck and a sign for me to give up on Miriam since I'd already reached my goal. My heart had decided, though— Miriam or no one. She became my do or die. Miriam had committed herself to me and her reaction when Raul showed up proved it. She erased all my pain. I even forgot about Jean-Baptiste. Instead of having anger and revenge consume me, I opened my heart to Miriam and let her sweet kisses console me. After all, forgiveness is proof of love.

Nothing Is Free

Miriam expressed a strong desire to find a job. She asked me to come over to her house to help her with her resume. On Saturday afternoon around two-thirty, I stopped by Miriam's house after work. I worked at the bank Monday through Friday from eight a.m. to six p.m., and every other Saturday from eight a.m. to one-thirty p.m.

Miriam opened the door; I walked in and took her in my embrace right away. Having her body against my chest felt so good. She squeezed my hips as I kissed her lips. As she leaned her head against my chest, I couldn't resist the grapefruit and bergamot scent of her wet hair. She had just washed it. I inhaled, and her aroma caught me off guard. I gently bit at her wet hair a few times, yet that wasn't enough. I kissed her neck and whispered into her ear, "You smell soooo good. I want to biiite you."

"Do as you please," Miriam said in a soothing voice.

"Where's Judith?" I asked as I kissed her more.

"She's bringing lunch to Mona."

I kissed her lips and let my hands slide down to her ass. I grabbed her buttocks just to discover she had no panties on. I knelt down and slipped my fingers down the soft skin of her legs before I turned her skirt into a veil. That peach fragrance again. I bit her fresh-shaved labia and licked her clit. I heard her sigh before she caressed my head with her hands. I raised my hands to reach the mound of her breasts and rolled them with my fingertips. Her moan sounded like a sweet cry and increased as I provided her with good pleasure. Miriam grabbed my head and pressed it against her labia even harder.

"Don't stop, babe. I'm coming," Miriam hissed before she trembled and exploded.

I bit the inside of her legs delicately and then I stood up, unbuckled my black belt and let my navy-blue pants and sky-blue boxers drop onto the floor before I sat on the couch. Miriam knelt in front of me, grabbed my lollipop, and took me to another universe. I leaned my head on the head of the couch and caressed her hair with my left hand, extending my right arm on the top of the couch. I had a million reasons to fall in love with Miriam.

All scary thoughts of being caught by Raul or Mona disappeared from my mind. A few minutes later, Miriam straddled me and moved her hips gracefully. I wrestled to maintain control over my body and not ejaculate before she was fully satisfied. Miriam put her left hand on my right shoulder and her right hand on my left leg to get some equilibrium as she squatted on my torch. "Oh my god! Yes! Yes! I'm coming, baby," she muttered as she went faster to that out-of-body experience.

"I'm coming with you, angel! I'm coming with you," I mumbled as I slapped her ass cheeks.

Upon satisfaction, Miriam leaned her head against my chest, and I kissed her hair. "Nothing is free in this world. Even for a resume you have to pay in advance," Miriam joked.

"We should do a new resume every week," I replied.

"I'll be broke," she said.

"I don't think so. You have an everlasting fortune."

"Go get detergent to wash the couch," Miriam said at the sight of semen on the sofa. "I just showered," she added after glancing between her legs and catching sight of dripping semen.

Miriam gave me a box of tissues she had by the TV stand before she walked into the bathroom. I stood up, got dressed, and then wiped the sofa. She washed up and changed her clothes. When Miriam came back, she kissed me, sat next to me, and opened her laptop. Not two minutes later, Judith came back. She greeted me, and I pinched her nose. I believe she had been outside all this time.

As Miriam and I focused on the resume, the door opened, and Raul walked in.

"Oh, I didn't know you were still coming here," Raul said to me as he stood in the doorway.

"I asked him to," Miriam snapped.

Raul glanced at the living room table and saw Miriam and me working on her resume. With his eyes, he scanned me from the top to the bottom and spotted the logo of the bank on my white t-shirt. Raul looked surprised. I guessed he didn't know I was a teller. "Why would you want to work at a bank when you could work at my office and make more money," Raul said to Miriam.

"There's an opening at your job?" Miriam asked.

"I could fire my secretary and hire you."

"Why didn't you do that before? I always told you I wanted to work, but you keep telling me I have no need of it."

Her answer hit Raul like a ton of bricks. "I'll be in your room," he said and then removed himself from the living room.

I waited fifteen more minutes before telling Miriam I was going home. She didn't welcome the idea. Miriam wanted me to stay with her in the living room while Raul was waiting for her. I believed sooner or later Raul would catch us. It was a matter of timing, but I was ready.

Miriam and I kept seeing each other at least twice a week at a cyber café located two blocks from her house. She was always with Judith at the cyber café. I would meet her inside and spend time with her. Although I wanted to have sex with her all the time, being in each other's embrace or presence was the most important thing for both of us. We also made time to chat with Elizabeth via webcam.

One day, Elizabeth advised us that if we were serious about the relationship, I should visit Miriam at her house and face Mona. Miriam didn't pressure me on that matter, but I knew she was tired of our hide-and-seek liaison. Finally, I decided to face Mona, and she welcomed me very well. Mona accepted my visiting her daughter after I finished work. When it was seven-thirty then, and Mona knew Raul was on his way, she said to Miriam, "Let the kid go home. It's dark outside and he lives far."

I walked for about twenty minutes to reach my house. I didn't consider it far, but Mona was fair with me, and I respected that. Whenever Mona gave her favorite speech to Miriam, I would stand up and go home. Miriam would stroll with me a few yards away from her house, just for us to find a dark spot to kiss each other. We were in love and happy. Miriam would also visit me on the Saturdays that I didn't go to work. After she'd make me breakfast, we would listen to romantic songs while she lay on my bed. Miriam and I decided to no longer go to a hotel and deal with all the stress that came with it. I had to buy a new mattress so Miriam could finally have sex with me in my room.

One day, as Miriam lay down on my mattress, taking a nap, I leaned my back against the wall with my hands crossed on my chest and contemplated her beauty in that black thong and with no bra on. I had girlfriends, women I loved, but Miriam was the first one whose finger I wanted to put a ring on and call her my wife—the queen who would reign and rule the kingdom of my heart.

I realized how blessed I was. Love had found me again after all I had done to women's hearts. I wondered why women still loved me so. One thing I knew for sure, God had given me a second chance to watch over an angel. This time I wouldn't mess it up. Without saying so out loud, I pledged my honesty and sincerity to Miriam. I didn't want her to find out about my rendezvous with Rachelle, so I thought of telling her that I'd slept with her best friend.

"What? Why are you staring at me like that?" Miriam said in an affectionate tone as she rolled over and tried to open her eyes and fix her hair in a ponytail.

"I have a confession," I said.

"Go ahead. I'm listening."

"I never thought I was gonna fall in love with you."

"Me neither," she said with a smile.

"You've cured my heart. You've made me forget about all my past heartbreaks. I no longer need to sleep with a lot of women to feel satisfied. I've found everything I've ever dreamed of in you. You're all the comfort I need in love."

"I would rather live in a single room like this with you sharing precious moments and seeing love in each other's eyes than to be with anyone else," Miriam confessed.

I climbed into the bed, looked into her eyes, and then said, "Give me three months, and we'll move in together. It's November now—by February, we'll be together." *Rachelle's news could wait, enjoy the moment, Leito.*

Do Not Run

A motorcycle with two men, Ronald and Ali, stopped in front of Oswald Beaubrun College, a private elementary and high school where Jean-Baptiste's children attended classes. The night before, the captain called Ronald and told him that Jean-Baptiste was on vacation and would be driving his children to school every morning. He ordered Ronald to wait for the kids to be dropped off before making any move against Jean-Baptiste.

Ronald had a hard time following orders. He wanted to do things his way—kill Jean-Baptiste in front of the school. Ronald planned to fire a bullet into Jean-Baptiste's head as soon as Jean-Baptiste pulled over to drop his children off. Ronald leaned against a tree, wearing a hat that covered his face. Ali made a U-turn with the bike and waited across the street going in the opposite direction with the bike on and ready to take off once they completed their mission. Both Ronald and Ali were looking for a black Toyota 4Runner 2000, the car Jean-Baptiste drove.

The street in front of the school was narrow; cars were coming in both directions, and drivers stopping to drop passengers off created traffic. Everything seemed normal that Monday, November 9, 2009. Most of the students looked happy and some were chit-chatting with their friends, while parents were rushing to go back to work or home—the normal routine.

"Get out of the car, walk fast to the school, but don't run," Jean-Baptiste ordered his children when he caught sight of a handgun on the waist of a man who had ducked by a tree. The man looked suspicious. Jean-Baptiste could tell by his outfit that the man was definitely not a cop. Jean-Baptiste then recognized Ronald, the suspicious man with all the tattoos.

Leila and Hervé nodded before they opened the back door and complied with their father's order. As Leila and Hervé edged away from him and got closer to Ronald, Jean-Baptiste's heart hammered. "Fuck," he yelled in his car when he realized that he'd sent his children straight into the trap. He gripped his gun and kept his eyes focused on his children.

Jean-Baptiste scanned both sidewalks to figure out how he would run after Ronald if he kidnapped the children. *What if Ronald murders them the way he did Johanne, the twelve-year-old kid in front of her school?* Jean-Baptiste realized at that very moment he might have made the worse decision in his entire life.

After the kids entered the school gates safe and sound, Jean-Baptiste let out a huge sigh of relief. Thank God, neither Ronald nor Ali knew the faces of Jean-Baptiste's children.

About three minutes later, several drivers created a commotion a few feet away from the school by honking at the driver of the black Toyota 4Runner who wouldn't move his vehicle. With a wink, Ronald signaled Ali to go and check on the black Toyota.

Ali drove calmly toward the car. He glanced inside of it and saw nobody. Ali scanned his surroundings to catch sight of Jean-Baptiste, and yet nothing.

"Ronald," Jean-Baptiste called out.

Ronald turned his head, and Jean-Baptiste fired one bullet in each cardinal point, north, south, west, and east. Pedestrians, students, drivers—they all ducked at the sound of gunfire. Stunned that Jean-Baptiste was aware of his presence, Ronald ran away in fear. Jean-Baptiste chased him. Ronald fired a couple of bullets toward Jean-Baptiste, who took cover, but continued pursuing him.

Jean-Baptiste had completed the first step, but he needed to shoot Ronald's shadow twice before he could kill him. He knew that a moving target represented a challenge for any shooter. He fired a few shots at Ronald's shadow, but missed the target. Jean-Baptiste believed it was now or never to kill Ronald.

As Ronald tried to escape, a young man running in the opposite direction bumped into him. Ronald shot him instantly—dead. The bullet lodged straight in the young man's heart. Ronald ran into a side street, and Jean-Baptiste lost sight of him.

Jean-Baptiste scanned the area and saw a young man dead on the ground. While tiptoeing after his target, Jean-Baptiste's heart stopped when he heard Ronald say, "Are you looking for me?"

Jean-Baptiste added no words and put his hands in the air.

"Let me see your face before I kill you."

Jean-Baptiste turned around slowly and his gaze met Ronald's. Ronald aimed at Jean-Baptiste's head and pulled the trigger twice—no more ammunition. As Ronald kept pulling the trigger of his Colt 45 with the hope of one last bullet remaining, Jean-Baptiste fired twice at Ronald's shadow before he lodged a bullet into Bloody Eyes' heart. Ronald fell on the ground—dead.

"If we meet again in hell, you'll be blind, motherfucker," Jean-Baptiste said before he put one bullet in each of Ronald's eye sockets. Jean-Baptiste breathed out heavily as he stared at his victim, the first man he'd ever killed in his life. His hands and feet became wet with perspiration.

While dealing with the brothers, Jean-Baptiste had come close to death twice: when he met Claude, and a few seconds before with Ronald.

"I killed Ronald Bloody Eyes, I killed Ronald Bloody Eyes," Jean-Baptiste roared as he dragged Ronald's corpse into the street.

As proud as he could be, Jean-Baptiste had, nonetheless, left another casualty by the school. One of the four bullets he'd fired previously killed a pedestrian. The action happened so fast that no witness could tell what exactly took place. The police department put the blame on Ronald. Patrick, the police commissioner, requested that they promote Jean-Baptiste immediately.

Are You Crazy?

On New Year's Eve, I went to Miriam's house around ten p.m. I'd rented a few DVDs of Haitian movies and brought a box of chocolates wrapped in a gift bag and two bottles of wine. I knocked at the door, and Miriam opened it for me. She pressed her lips against mine, and we twirled our tongues in each other's mouth. The bottles of wine and the box of chocolate prevented me from squeezing the flesh of her derriere. I loved to squeeze her butt.

At the sound of Mona's footsteps, we released each other. I stood by the couch as Miriam bent in front of her DVD player and inserted one of the DVDs I gave her. As soon as Mona walked into the living room, I greeted her with a kiss on the cheek and gave her the bottles.

"Mona doesn't drink alcohol, Leito," Miriam said before she grabbed the bottles.

"I'm sorry," I apologized to Mona.

"It's okay. You didn't know," Mona replied.

"Since you don't drink, take this then," I said to Mona as I handed her the box of chocolates I'd bought for Miriam.

"Oh! How come you gave Mona my gift?" Miriam asked in a joking way.

"You take the bottle, now I have the chocolates," Mona replied.

"Here's your bottles—give me my gift," Miriam joked.

Mona clung onto the gift and didn't let go. Miriam poked her mother playfully. Mona jerked. Miriam poked Mona more and Mona tried to run away. They laughed out loud. I was mesmerized by that amazing moment between Miriam and her mother. It was the first time I had seen Mona laugh. A twinge of sorrow caught me. I wished my mother were still alive and I could have played with her the way Miriam did with her mom.

I sat down on the couch, and Miriam lay on the couch as well with her head resting on my lap. I felt a little uncomfortable with Mona there, even though she was going back and forth in the kitchen. Mona was cooking a pumpkin soup. January 1st was the Independence Day of Haiti, and having pumpkin soup after midnight was one of our traditions. Around eleven-thirty, Mona went to the kitchen and didn't come back.

As we watched the movie, I glanced at Miriam's legs a couple of times, and my phallus poked against my boxers.

"Why is it poking me?" Miriam asked in a joking way.

I looked into her eyes and said, "Take off your panties."

"Are you crazy? Mona is right there in the kitchen," Miriam snapped.

I hypnotized her with my big brown eyes; Miriam shook her head and obeyed me. I caressed her legs, and she panted. I swirled my middle fingertip on her clit. Miriam sighed and then closed her eyes. I swirled my finger and inserted it into her vagina. Miriam jerked each time I inserted my finger inside her. Once I felt her spasms on my finger, I inserted my left hand inside her dress and rolled her hard nipples. She rolled her waist and moaned in a hissed voice. Her convulsions increased; she whined more and then let out a deep breath after she exploded.

"That felt so good, baby," Miriam muttered.

I stood up, walked to the door, and then said, "Come."

Miriam shot a glance at me, obviously wondering what my intentions were. Then she sprang from the couch and came to me. I felt the urge to penetrate her. I positioned her in the middle of the door facing the kitchen where Mona was cooking the soup.

I stood behind Miriam, and whispered in her ear, "I want to end this year and start the New Year inside of you." Miriam added no words. She simply opened her legs. I lifted her dress, unzipped my pants, and penetrated her. She quivered.

Every time I thrust into her, I felt as though it were the first time I'd ever penetrated a woman. Her wet vagina drove me crazy. I wanted to stay longer, but the sensation caused by the convulsions of Miriam's vagina around my penis had decided the opposite. I grabbed her waist, I thrust into her, pulled out, thrust into her, pulled out. Miriam couldn't resist the sensation. She extended her arms to reach and grip each side of the door frame. Her moaning became audible. I thrust into her, pulled out, thrust into her, and my knees shivered after I climaxed.

"Miriam," Mona called out seconds later. We heard her footsteps heading toward us.

"Yes, Mom," Miriam replied and quickly walked to meet her mom halfway so I could pull up my pants and hide her panties that were on the couch.

"Come and taste the soup and tell me if it's good," Mona said.

Miriam followed her mother into the kitchen and came back a few minutes later to invite me into the dining room for the soup. "Your sperm is dripping down my legs," she whispered.

"Let it dry out," I said before I gave Miriam a soft slap on the butt and squeezed her flesh. Miriam shook her head and comprehended that she would have to put up with a lot of craziness on my side. I kissed Mona on the cheeks and wished her all the best for the New Year before taking a seat at the table. We enjoyed a good time in the dining room. The pumpkin soup was delicious.

That was the best New Year's Eve and New Year's Day I ever had. I didn't go to any parties, but I would have chosen this way of celebrating for the rest of my life. Miriam and I hadn't spent Christmas together because she'd visited her grandparents in Cotes-de-Fer with Mona and Judith. Judith then stayed with her parents for a few more weeks and would be back on January 15th.

Repent

During my first week at the accounting firm, they assigned me to do an external audit at an international non-governmental organization on Bourdon Road. That Tuesday, January 12, 2010, was my second day auditing the files. By ten in the morning, I heard some employees talking about a woman arrested by the local police in Léogane, a city located about twenty-two miles away from Port-au-Prince. The woman was carrying a bag that contained the heads of ten children. They stated she'd sacrificed those children to obtain winning lottery numbers. I wanted to ask them where that woman found those ten babies' heads, but I kept my question to myself.

Elie Jerome

Around three-thirty p.m., my phone rang and I picked it up.

"How's your day going, my love?" Miriam asked.

"So far, so good, and yours?" I replied.

"I'm okay. I have a gift for you. Will you stop by after work?"

"Thank you angel. What kind of gift is it?" I asked.

"It's a surprise. I'm waiting for you. I love you."

"I adore you, angel," I said before I hung up. Hearing Miriam's sweet voice always felt good; it boosted my energy. Rumor or fact, I didn't bother to tell Miriam about the woman the police had arrested with the ten babies' heads in a bag.

As I was making copies of some financial documents, the copy machine stopped. I examined the machine; everything looked good, but it wouldn't make any more copies. Since it was already four p.m., I packed up my documents and headed out.

"Be careful. They just assassinated one of the professors at the public university," the guard said.

"What's going on? I heard they caught a woman with ten babies' heads in a bag, and now an assassination," I replied.

"Only God knows," the guard said with a shrug. I headed to the main road and caught a bus. A few minutes after I took a seat, the thought of Miriam's surprise gift for me came to my mind. I guessed about all types of gifts I might receive from her, and yet I was still intrigued. But an abrupt and strong ground-shaking jerked me out of my imaginings and brought me back to reality. *What kind of concrete drill are they using to build the road?* I asked myself. The bus stopped in the intersection of Lalue and Avenue Christophe.

All the passengers, including me, glanced at each other in confusion with the hope that one of us could explain the strong shaking of the ground. Seconds later, we heard a loud scream, dust surrounded us, and we couldn't see further than two feet in front of us. Everyone including the driver got off the bus and ran.

The dust became thicker and limited my vision to the point of my nose. Since I was aware of the tense and hostile political climate within the country, I thought maybe someone had planted a bomb near the National Palace. I didn't panic, but I was afraid that I had taken the wrong direction and might bump right into the chaos. I tried to run and ran into two people. "What's going on?" I asked the second person.

"Earthquake, earthquake," he said in a distressed voice before disappearing into the dust. *Earthquake?* The first and last quake I'd experienced was in August 2005, when I was at the house of my ex-girlfriend, Sherley. During that tremor in August 2005, Sherley clung to me, and I laughed. I found the tremor beneath my feet amusing. From that experience I could never have pictured an earthquake as a hazard capable of causing such strong damage to human lives and properties.

When the dust became thinner and my vision cleared, I glanced around and muttered, "Holy shit!" All the houses on the entire block where I stood had collapsed. I freaked out, and my knees trembled. I saw a female student crawling out from a collapsed school building.

"Help me, help me," she begged.

I stood frozen in front of her as my brain tried to recollect the definition of the word *Help*. I found myself with a dilemma. Should I run like everybody else to find my family, or should I rescue that student? Once I regained my composure, I leaned toward her and tried to help her stand.

"I can't. My…my… my…other leg….. Other leg is under the wall," she stammered.

I looked at the wall and I would definitely need a super power to remove her leg from under it, or I would need to hammer the wall down. *Where would I find that hammer?* I panicked. I'd trained at the Haitian Red Cross, but nothing about rescuing people was mentioned during those classes. Now, I spotted a huge piece of round steel; I slid it under the wall. I pulled, I pulled, I pulled with all my guts and soul, yet the wall didn't flinch an inch. The ground shook one more time. I sprinted into the street.

"Repent, repent, it's the end of time," a man shouted as he was running.

I looked the student in her eyes one last time, shook my head, and ran away. *Will you let her die, Leito?* my heart asked me each step of the way while I edged away from the student in distress. Half a block away, I made a U-turn and came back to help. I grabbed the piece of steel and lifted it as much as I could, but still with no result. A few seconds later, two other hands grabbed the steel, and we lifted the wall off of her leg.

"Thanks," I said to the man who'd helped me save the student. The man and I carried the student away from the building. The man looked as though he had plunged his body in a bag of beige sand. No need for a mirror, the man's face gave me an idea of how my own face looked at that moment.

"Venel, Venel, Venel," the student called out.

"Who's Venel?" I asked.

"My little brother, my little brother," she replied as she pointed to the collapsed building. I shot a look at the man. We both acknowledged we saw no sign of life. The school had collapsed with all the students and staff—leaving behind no survivors other than the girl we'd rescued.

"God is with you. I gotta go," I said to the student who nodded while weeping in pain and calling out her little brother's name.

"I live across the street. I'll attend to her needs," the man said.

Like ants, people were screaming and running in all directions. On my way home, I saw that the National Palace and many other federal buildings had collapsed, including the National Penitentiary, which had allowed many convicts to escape. In no time, I was already in Martissant 15, where I spotted a gas station on fire in Martissant 19. Less than fifteen seconds later, a propane tank from the gas station bounced everywhere and headed in my direction. People screamed. "Let's go into that alley," someone shouted.

I quickly entered the alley and ran. I saw people standing and watching as the tank continued on its path. I was no journalist. I knew I'd rather read the newspaper than die while trying to catch the scene. On my way home, I stopped at family and friends' houses to check on them. Thank God, they were all okay.

Along the way, people said the same things to their friends and family members, "Thank God, you're still alive. Did you see X and Y? What about Z?" Some answers were positive and others negative. Everyone wanted to go home and check on their family.

I continued my marathon and along the way witnessed people covered with dust, bleeding and screaming for help. Dead bodies lay on the sidewalks. Cars were parked, pointing in all directions. Finally, I reached home. My entire family was safe and sound. We hugged each other like never before and said, "Thank you, Jesus." I didn't check on Jean-Baptiste because though I knew he was in town, we had stopped speaking to each other since the night he'd slapped me in the face.

I sprinted to Cote Plage 26. As soon as I entered the block, my knees quivered, and I felt something inside of me drop away. I lost my strength all of a sudden. My palpitations increased, and I feared the worse. I didn't know what the problem was, but I couldn't catch my breath. A few feet away, I spotted a pancake—Miriam's house. I trudged; bad news was waiting for me, and I didn't intend to rush to hear it.

"I killed Miriam," Mona cried out in agony with her arms open toward me.

I took her in my embrace, and stared at the collapsed house. My heart stopped when I saw Miriam's left hand extended out—the only visible part of her body underneath the huge concrete roof that had fallen on her. I didn't know if it was me or Mona or both of us, but our bodies shuddered against each other.

"I killed Miriam, I killed Miriam, I killed Miriam," Mona continued.

"It wasn't you, Mona. It was the earthquake," one of the neighbors said as she rubbed Mona's back before she wrapped a piece of clothing tightly around Mona's waist to give her strength to bear the gut-wrenching pain caused by the loss of her only daughter.

I took Mona's hands, and we sat down in the street. I remained speechless. My eyes were filled with tears and my heart ached.

"Oh! Oh! Oh! Look how I killed Miriam. Oh! Oh! Oh! Look how I killed my only daughter," Mona repeated as she stomped her right foot and stared at the collapsed house.

"Why do you say that you killed Miriam?" I asked Mona.

Mona looked into my eyes. She didn't have to give me an answer, but at the same time she felt I deserved to know the truth. "I was outside, and Miriam came up to me and said that she was pregnant with your child. I snapped and asked her to leave the house right away." Mona shook her head, as more tears rolled down her cheeks and continued, "Miriam walked inside, and the house collapsed." Mona stood up and screamed, "Miriam! Miriam! Miriam!" before she rolled over on the ground. I wrestled to hold her, and another neighbor helped me.

"Miriam, Miriam, what will I do without you? Oh Lord, take me instead!" Mona revealed the secret gift Miriam had for me.

I stood up, moved to the collapsed house, and touched Miriam's hand searching for a pulse. Maybe in denial, I found her hand warm, so I started moving away huge pieces of concrete. *Miriam could still be alive*, I convinced myself.

"Leito, she's dead," Mona said.

I closed my ears to Mona's comment. Dead or alive, I wanted to take Miriam in my embrace one last time. Some of the men from the neighborhood joined me with hammers and pickaxes. We created a space and removed Miriam's body from the rubble. I swooned at the sight of her dead body.

As I sat in the rubble, I took Miriam in my embrace, and held her there. I pictured me holding Miriam in my arms, kissing her all over her body to express my happiness after she told me she was carrying my child. My throat muscles tightened. I looked at the sky—a dark and sad sky. Later, I didn't recall seeing any stars in the sky that night. My sinful life didn't stop me from begging God for grace. *God, please save her, please save her. God, please have mercy,* my heart cried out. I breathed air into her nose. I cut my finger and put my blood on her lips. Like in the movies, I hoped to resuscitate her—but nothing.

Throughout the entire city, victims were being rescued. Rescue teams went under collapsed homes and buildings and saved as many people as possible. As it got darker, and the ground kept shaking, they stopped the search and rescue missions. Everyone camped in open fields, in the middle of the streets, or on school playgrounds to wait for dawn.

While waiting for dawn, some Christians chanted songs that brought mental strength to all. Christians claimed the event as a sign of the end of times. Since we had no communication with the outside world, many thought the quake had occurred all over the world. A few people speculated that a third world war had started, thinking that Russia had bombed all the Caribbean countries.

I had no idea how I would be able to recover from this loss; the only woman I'd loved had died. I found no good in life since everyone I loved had died: my mom, my grandmother, my grandfather, my cousin James, and now Miriam. Maybe I was cursed to only taste love, but to never enjoy it in its fullness for the rest of my life.

A Coincidence

Claude was among the convicts who escaped when the walls of the prison fell. Besides being one of the most notorious criminals the country had ever known, Claude was a smart man. After the death of his brother, while still in prison, Claude asked the people in the slum he helped to open businesses to inquire about Jean-Baptiste. He became aware that Jean-Baptiste was the son-in-law of the police commissioner. So after liberating himself from prison, Claude stole a bike and headed to Paco, where the police commissioner lived.

Around three-thirty in the morning, Claude reached his destination and found the police commissioner trapped with both legs under a huge concrete wall. "Thank God you're here," the police commissioner (a.k.a the captain) said when he caught sight of Claude. In a normal situation, the police commissioner would have said, "How the hell did you find my house?"

Claude glared at the police commissioner.

"What?" the police commissioner asked.

"What!' Claude said before he giggled and shook his head. "Your son-in-law had me arrested the day I told you it was gonna be my last job and I would leave the country."

"It was a coincidence, I had nothing to do with that," the police commissioner pleaded.

"Oh… a coincidence… But you sent him to another city when you knew my brother was going after him."

"What did you want me to do? My daughter needs her husband."

"Oh, I see… You care for your daughter, but you don't give a shit about us besides having us kill for you and make you rich."

"Listen, Claude, I understand how you feel. Help me and I'll make sure you leave the country."

"That's funny. How will I be able to leave the country when I just escaped death in prison and your son-in-law killed my brother?"

"I have money. I'll give it to you."

"I can't trust you. Tell me where the money is, and I'll help you," Claude said.

"Okay, okay, you see that old car. Go inside, slide your hand underneath the back seats, and you'll feel a zipper. The money is there."

Claude walked toward the old car in the garage and did as the police commissioner told him. He found a lot of cash, more than three-hundred-thousand dollars in US currency in rolls of fifty and hundred dollar bills. Claude put the money in a bag and then returned to the police commissioner.

"What do you want me to do with all that money, Captain?" Claude asked.

"Take as much as you want and leave me some."

"I need a gun now," Claude added.

"What do you need it for?" Claude shot a glance at the police commissioner.

"You'll find some guns inside the garage in a big tool box. Both of my legs are ruined. I can't take the pain any longer. You gotta help me." The police commissioner groaned in pain.

"Okay, Captain," Claude said before he grabbed a huge piece of concrete and dropped it on the police commissioner's head. "That's for my brother," Claude said before he lifted the concrete and dropped it on the captain's

head one more time, "That's for getting me arrested."
Claude took the guns and the money and disappeared.

Jesus! Jesus! Jesus!

At dawn, I left Mona and rejoined my family. The light of the sun disclosed the damage caused by the earthquake. All the houses seemed to have collapsed like pancakes. People were lying dead or trapped underneath huge slabs of concrete like ham and cheese sandwiches. Blood could be seen everywhere, along with mutilated body parts, and broken bones. I shook my head in denial. *This can't be true. I must be dreaming.* Only in movies, did they show such horrible scenes of such a large scale of destruction. I closed my eyes, then opened them with the hope that the scenery would change; yet it remained the same.

People were crying over the loss of their loved ones, while others were running to find missing family members and friends. I heard later that when groups tried looting the local banks and supermarkets, security guards fired their weapons at them. The magnitude of the quake knocked out the entire city. Law enforcement officers, firefighters, doctors, and nurses were nowhere to be found.

Before I returned to my family, I decided to check on Margaret and her family. Twenty yards away, I noticed Margaret's house was gone. Only a square concrete basin built on the rooftop to provide water to the house remained standing on the spot. The ground seemed to have swallowed up her entire house. I thought despair would stop me dead in my tracks, but instead, I regained my strength and ran faster.

"I'm killing myself. Let me kill myself... Let me kill myself," Jean-Baptiste shouted while holding his handgun, and neighbors wrestled with him to take the gun away. Jean-Baptiste wanted to commit suicide. The neighbors had enough on their plates, yet they begged Jean-Baptiste to not pull the trigger.

"Here's Leito," a neighbor said aloud.

"Leito, Leito, can you convince Jean-Baptiste to drop his gun. He wants to kill himself," Junior yelled once he caught sight of me about ten feet away from Jean-Baptiste.

"Let the coward kill himself," I said when Jean-Baptiste's eyes met mine. The neighbors glanced at me in confusion. They didn't expect such a comment from me. "I need a few men to help me go underneath the rubble. They might still be alive," I added.

"Let me go get my hammer," said Kinas, one of the neighbors.

Jean-Baptiste removed the ammunition from his gun and handed it to an elderly woman. He leaned against a tree and wept uncontrollably. A few minutes later, some brave neighbors surrounded me and we started hammering on the visible part of the rooftop. The concrete was too thick to penetrate, so we changed our plan. With a shovel and a pickaxe, we dug around and created a gap to go inside the house that was buried in the ground. Kinas volunteered to go inside.

Kinas came back out right away and said, "I need a flashlight." He received it in a matter of seconds. He went deeper, and we lost sight of the flashlight.

"Did you see anyone?' I asked Kinas aloud. I received no answer. My heart pounded, and I became anxious. I wanted to go after Kinas, but I needed a flashlight.

A few minutes later, I heard someone coughing. It sounded like a child. Kinas carried out Hervé. Jean-Baptiste sprinted toward Hervé, grabbed his son, and held him tightly in his arms.

"God is able," a neighbor said to Jean-Baptiste before she patted him on his back. "In the name of Jesus, your family will be safe and sound," she added as she worshiped God with songs and waving her hands in the air.

"I need to drink some water before I go back inside again. The dust is killing me," Kinas said.

"Let me go inside now," I suggested.

"I already know how it looks inside so finding them will be easier for me," Kinas replied. Junior handed Kinas a cup of water. Kinas sipped on the water, took a deep breath, and then went underneath the debris again. This time, Kinas came back with empty hands. We all glanced at him, and he shook his head.

"Margaret is dead. She was in the kitchen. When the house collapsed, the concrete wall fell over the fridge and it probably killed her right away," Kinas told us before he cupped his face in both hands.

I couldn't believe what he said. I grabbed the flashlight and jumped into the little gap to witness the truth myself. Maybe Margaret still had a pulse. It was pitch black in there, and without a flashlight, seeing anything would be impossible. I'd just passed the living room, and I started suffocating due to the heavy dust. I removed my shirt and covered my nose with it to help me breathe in less dust. I saw the door of the refrigerator that had hit Margaret's back and had broken her spine. I touched her hand, which was cold. I touched her neck, no pulse. I put my hand on her heart, no heartbeat.

I strode out, but before I exited, I heard a sneeze. My heart jumped. I turned around and tried to detect where the sneeze came from.

"Leila, Leila, Margaret, Margaret," I called out, and yet I received no answer. Each time I opened my mouth, more dust entered my lungs. I understood why Kinas never answered us when he was inside. I sprinted back out to catch my breath. "I heard a sneeze inside, but I couldn't see where it came from," I said to the other neighbors who were anxiously waiting outside.

Kinas grabbed the flashlight from my hands and jumped into the gap.

"Leila," I called out when I saw the tip of her head coming out. She was covered with dust. I took her in my embrace as though she were my own child. Leila represented a miracle for all. She suffered from asthma, and no one would have believed that she could have survived for hours underneath the debris in that dusty environment. I gave Leila to her sobbing father.

The whole neighborhood turned into search-and-rescue teams comprised of family members, friends, neighbors, and good Samaritans who risked their lives to save others. As the angel of death was grabbing souls, brave men were hammering down walls, women were praying to God, and survivors were fighting with death itself.

Our ancestors fought Napoleon Bonaparte's army, the greatest army at that time. Now, we were fighting an earthquake with non-stop strong aftershocks that kept bringing more buildings down. Fatigue and lack of food combined couldn't slow the power of the hammers against these concrete walls.

Those who survived came out covered with dust, bloody and with broken bones. Not all families were fortunate, however. Some lost everyone and everything— the entire family exterminated. The more fortunate families found comfort and strength in saying, "The Lord giveth and the Lord taketh away. Blessed be the name of the Lord."

We all witnessed acts of bravery, love, faith, resilience, brotherhood, and sorrow. Survivors told their stories of how they were able to escape death. Those same survivors informed the rescuers about others caught under the rubble. People were diligent in responding to the needs of the rescuers as well as the survivors.

"I was talking to X, Y, Z last night, and I didn't hear anything from them this morning," some survivors explained. Since more survivors were coming out alive, people's faith in the possibility of the missing surviving grew stronger. Due to the lack of adequate equipment, some victims had to shelter in place underneath the debris. The rescuers provided them with food and water.

While crying and chanting songs to God, the Haitian women managed to cook for the rescuers. They used wood from the debris as charcoal to cook. Everyone brought whatever goods they were able to spare. One cup of hot coffee might be served as breakfast and people would feel lucky if it was served with bread.

Each neighborhood saw the same type of scene and the same battle, men against death. Some people rescued only minutes before died in front of their families due to internal bleeding or failed organs. Some survivors requested drinking water, and as soon as it was given to them, they died. The news spread within the neighborhoods in seconds: Don't give liquids to the survivors. Soak a piece of clean cloth with water and press it against the lips of the victims. Many believed the liquid precipitated the death of the victims who already had internal injuries.

Whether this was fact or fiction, we spread the word, but no physician was available to confirm this statement.

A clothing factory had been situated about thirty yards from my house. Half of the building collapsed on its employees, killing and injuring many. Some employees trapped under the rubble asked rescuers to amputate their legs and move them away from the building, as the walls kept falling following each aftershock. They'd rather live without one or both legs than be dead. So the rescuers used hacksaws and cut off the legs of three individuals and got them out. They cut their legs without making tourniquets for them, and minutes later, those people bled to death.

Fear or faith, everyone called out, "Jesus! Jesus! Jesus!" whenever the ground shook. I didn't recall people calling upon any other god, but the name of Jesus. The survivors acknowledged the power of Jesus.

After seeing dead bodies all over the place, sleeping that night represented a challenge for me. As I lay on the ground in the street like everybody else, I stared at the sky and reminisced about the great moments I'd spent with Miriam. With my heart in anguish and tears flowing down my face, I waited impatiently for slumber to take me away from my suffering. If Miriam hadn't moved from the neighborhood, maybe she would have lived. The house she'd rented near me had remained standing.

Born in It, Die in It

The next day, the battle to save lives continued. Cops regrouped to provide security to the public. The injured were transported to hospitals and clinics in wheelbarrows, on backs, and over the heads of friends and family members. Many hospitals were completely destroyed; the few that had withstood the tremor were without staff and medication to respond to the needs of the injured. Some doctors and nurses walked miles by foot to reach the healthcare facilities they were working at while others provided onsite care to the injured in their neighborhoods.

With their bare hands, doctors and nurses were saving lives. More wounded were coming, and the medical staff felt overwhelmed. Even before the quake, the medical staff didn't have enough equipment to provide adequate healthcare to the people; after the earthquake it was even worse.

I took a bike and rode from Carrefour to the main city. Everything lined up for us to think the earthquake was an apocalypse. The National Palace and many other federal buildings were destroyed. Big churches and voodoo temples stood in ruins. All the motels where the prostitutes worked in Grand Rue on the Jean Jacques Dessalines Boulevard were debris.

I spotted a commotion where many people stood by a collapsed motel. I moved closer with my bike and saw a dead man kneeling with his head in between the legs of a woman. The ceiling had fallen on the woman, leaving her legs in a V-shape as the only visible part of her body.

"This guy had the best death ever, in a pussy. Born in it, die in it," one of the pedestrians said.

That dead couple in the motel became the highlight of the earthquake. People walked miles to come and see them. I heard a ton of speculation about that couple. Many people claimed they knew the man. The ability of Haitians to create stories and conjecture about a man and a woman always fascinated me.

I rode to a couple of other neighborhoods to see the impact of the quake, and I also checked on some friends to make sure they were still alive. I heard stories of people who'd escaped the first fifteen seconds of the quake, but then went back inside their homes to grab their phones and perished. I wanted to slap those idiots. When I went to Bourdon Road to the non-governmental organization building where I was working, I saw that half of the building had been destroyed. Around five p.m., I reached home.

As I leaned against a tree and tried to comprehend how all the damage could have been minimized, I realized more lives could have been saved if other cities that weren't affected by the earthquake could have brought some help. The quake hit Port-au-Prince and its surrounding cities, but we felt as though the whole country had been destroyed. Every single function of the state was centralized in Port-au-Prince. I heard stories of people who died because they'd left their cities to go to Port-au-Prince for a passport or an ID.

The earthquake brought to light the lack of infrastructure in Haiti. Too many houses were built without building codes. The ground shook; it brought everything down and killed thousands of people. The majority of houses in Port-au-Prince had one entrance and exit, no back door. Some victims could have escaped death, but by the time they ran all the way from the back of their houses to the exit in the front, it was too late.

At dusk, I glanced around and watched the unity among all of us. Rich, poor, educated, illiterate, we all slept next to each other in the streets, eating together. It saddened me to see that Haitians had to wait for a disaster to understand that we were one nation. Blame all of it on our educational system that was supposed to develop and strengthen the country, but instead divided us. Like all Haitian kids, the first book I was introduced to at school was called Ti Malice (*Little Malice*), and no need for me to go over the meaning of the word malice.

They injected in our brain stories about Bouki and Ti Malice, two Haitian fictional characters who shaped the mind of the nation from generation to generation. They depicted Bouki as an illiterate, the one who always discovered treasures and called upon Ti Malice to share the treasures with him. Ti Malice, the educated one, would take everything for himself and get *Bouki* in trouble with the authorities. Regardless of how many times Ti Malice betrayed Bouki, Bouki would still trust him. Those stories taught us tricking one another is smarter than working with each other. Bouki and Ti Malice stories created a lack of trust within the society and killed the spirit of true friendship and patriotism.

The majority of the Haitian voters had never set foot into a school. They elected candidates emotionally in the hope of a better tomorrow. Those candidates who were educated and who should work for the benefit of the people cared only for themselves, and let the country be engulfed in misery day after day. To understand this simple fact, call a Haitian Bouki and you'll see the difference in their facial expression compared to if you call them Ti Malice.

Flesh and Blood

Early the next morning, I was having some coffee; Jean-Baptiste came and sat next to me. "Did you know Margaret was your number one fan?" he said.

"Nice try," I replied with a giggle.

"I'm serious. She said she loved the way you played ball. Sometimes, she teased me saying if she had met you before me, she would have dated you."

I nodded as I reminisced on those good old days playing soccer and the love I received from the fans. Some called me Ronaldo, others Recoba or Materazzi. It all depended on my position on the field. Anytime I had a chance to go and replay good moments of my past I jumped at the opportunity. It was the best and only mental escape I had after the disaster.

"I saw your conquest of women, and knowing that she liked you so much drove me nuts," Jean-Baptiste added.

"Do you think I would do something like that to you?" I asked.

"Hey, you're flesh and blood."

I sipped on my coffee and didn't bother to answer him. Anger was burning inside of me, and I wanted to throw the hot coffee in his face. I still yearned for my revenge.

Jean-Baptiste rubbed his hands together and then said, "Many convicts escaped from prisons. They're killing cops non-stop and raping women at night. I have to go back to work."

"What does this have to do with me?" I asked.

"I need your help with the kids. Margaret's father was killed, and you're the only family they have. You're the only one I trust my kids with," Jean-Baptiste said.

"Wow, that's cute. Last time I helped your family, you slapped me and tried to take me to jail."

"You can slap me back. I admit it—I was stupid," Jean-Baptiste apologized.

"I'll forgive you only if you let me smack you with a hammer in your face," I replied as I turned my head and made eye contact with him.

Jean-Baptiste sighed, stood up, and walked away without saying a word. The wrinkles on my forehead explained clearly my feelings toward him. Halfway he stopped, turned around, and said, "You know Claude escaped from prison. He and his crew are terrorizing the city again. They already assassinated nine cops." Jean-Baptiste removed himself without receiving any comment from me regarding his last sentence.

I wanted to tell him to go fuck himself. I saved his life and his kids, but he never thanked me. Jean-Baptiste knew about Miriam, and he didn't even try to say anything about my loss. He gave me so many reasons to hate him.

Before dusk, I saw Junior coming with Hervé and Leila.

"Where are you going with the kids?" I called out with my arms in the air.

"Jean-Baptiste told me they were staying with us tonight, and he spoke to you already," Junior replied.

"Jean-Baptiste asked me, and I told him no. Bring the kids back to their father," I yelled.

Junior stopped halfway and stared at me. He looked confused about my reaction. "Let's go back to your father," he said to the kids.

"You don't love us anymore, Uncle Leito?" Leila asked me with an innocent voice that reminded me the voice of Margaret, her mother. Leila took a puff from her asthma inhaler and kept her eyes on mine while waiting for my answer.

"Yes, I do love you, guys," I replied.

"So why don't you want us to stay with you?" Leila asked.

"I'm just kidding. I was pranking Junior," I lied with a smile.

Leila and Hervé ran into my arms, and I kissed them each on the forehead. If I explained to Leila the reason I didn't want to keep them, I would have to give Junior an explanation about the incident between Jean-Baptiste and me. The slap in my face remained like a fresh wound in my heart, and I was ashamed to talk about it.

As we lay on a comforter in the streets, Hervé asked me, "Where's my mother, Uncle Leito?"

"Your mother is an angel. Now she's gone to heaven," I replied.

After that day, Hervé drew pictures of a woman with wings heading to the sky. Jean-Baptiste and I barely interacted with each other. Around two p.m., he picked up his kids and sent them back by dusk before returning to his duties. Jean-Baptiste slept at the house of Nahomi, his cousin. At night, gunshots echoed everywhere. At dawn, we would see men lying dead on the ground in their own blood.

Gone Forever

After the disaster, everyone thought there'd be a new beginning for the country. When people heard about the convicts who had escaped from the prisons, some of them said they were happy that those convicts made it out alive and hoped the earthquake would have set them on different path of life. Other people remained skeptical and considered those outlaws as threats to the community. Two days after the quake, many cases of rape and murder were reported throughout the city. Besides the captain, however, Claude had killed no one else after he escaped from prison. But since he was the most notorious criminal among the escaped, they blamed all the crimes committed by the other felons on Claude.

At dawn, Claude reached the slum where he'd lived before he got arrested. He stopped by Ali's house, and Ali was more than happy to see him again. Ali explained to Claude the incident that had happened when the cops came in, shattered the slum, and killed seventeen young men. Claude told stories about his experience in the National Penitentiary.

"I'm not here to stay. I have two things to do, and I'll be gone forever," Claude said to Ali.

Claude's girlfriend, Sandra, was waiting for him in the Dominican Republic. The day he was arrested by Jean-Baptiste was supposed to be his last day in Haiti. Claude paid an employee at the immigration office to get his passport printed under someone else's name. He planned to go to the Dominican Republic and then fly from there to Panama with his girlfriend. Although Claude was skilled at committing crimes and making a lot of money from his illicit activities, he never liked the lifestyle. He dreamt of a normal life and having kids with his girlfriend.

"What do you have in mind?" Ali asked.

"I need to teach the chief of the prison a lesson," Claude replied.

"What happened with him?"

"This guy took pleasure in mistreating me. He beat me up every day. He made me wait for every other convict to eat before I could eat some leftovers. One day, a prisoner had diarrhea and shit all over the floor, the chief had me clean up the mess with my bare hands."

"We'll make this motherfucker bleeeed," Ali growled. "I'll go with you to finish him off once and for all."

"I appreciate that, Ali, but that's none of your business. After all we've been through and since you survived that quake, I think you should start a new life somewhere else. This is your chance for a new beginning."

"I understand all you're saying, but I like what I am doing, man. It's exciting," Ali replied.

"How is killing people exciting for you? I did all of this because I had no choice. The Iron Teeth were after me and my brother, after they killed my mother. Just go to another country and start fresh. I'll give you money to get you out of here"

Ali shook his head. "It seems like jail got you soft. I'll take over if you're afraid. We have a lot of other recruits who believe in us."

"That's what I'm saying. We can become a new model for all of them. They'll follow us. I have enough money to help everyone start fresh," Claude said.

"What's the second plan?" Ali asked.

"Jean-Baptiste, the cop who arrested me and killed my brother. He's my next target."

"What about his friend, Leito?" Ali asked.

"I owe my life to this guy. Don't even think about touching him. If it wasn't for him, I have no clue where I'd be today. Leito was more than a brother to me and the greatest friend I ever had. For him, money meant nothing, just a piece of paper. Leito was the Santa to many. The guy was a kid, but he wouldn't let anyone go to sleep with an empty stomach. He would steal his parents' money and buy us shoes and clothes. He kept our hopes high. If you ask the few neighbors who knew him, they would tell you more about him. Leito helped everyone in need. Sometimes his parents caught him stealing their money and whipped him, but Leito never said who he helped with the money. Leito was like a safe, you could tell him any secret and he would take it to the grave. Many of us took him for granted and took advantage of his good heart. When his mother passed away, things changed. We all mourned the death of his mother because we suffered from her absence."

"Ronald didn't want to touch him, and you're afraid of him too."

"My brother told you about Leito?"

"Yes, he did, but I don't give a shit," Ali said.

"Let me ask you a question. What does the word gratitude mean to you?"

"I believe anything people did for me was just because they have their own interest in me. Even for God to save you, you have to give him your heart. Everything is about exchange. Call it what you want, but we don't get anything for free. If it wasn't for Leito, Ronald would have kidnapped Jean-Baptiste's wife and later on killed Jean-Baptiste. Ronald would have still been alive," Ali growled.

Claude remained silent and couldn't understand the reasons behind Ali's thirst to kill Leito. "I need to take a nap. Keep in mind I'm not here."

"When are we leaving?" Ali asked.

"We're going after the chief of the prison first. We'll depart at dusk."

Ali walked out and closed the door behind him, and Claude lay down to rest. Claude spent the entire day inside the room. Nobody knew about his presence, not even the other gang members. Ali brought him food and water. Around six p.m., Ali turned on his bike, and Claude sat behind him. They headed to the home of the chief of the prison.

When Claude and Ali got to the chief's house, it was pitch black. The majority of the citizens were already in the streets or the other open areas to spend the night. Wilfrid, the chief of the prison, and his wife were gathering their belongings before they went to sleep on the streets when Claude and Ali pulled a gun on them.

As Claude took aim at Wilfrid's head with his Taurus Judge, Ali walked behind Wilfrid and handcuffed him. Wilfrid's wife held her belly while she tried to catch her breath. She was shocked and panting, and also eight months pregnant.

Claude pulled down Wilfrid's pants and then put him on the floor. Claude kneeled with his left knee on Wilfrid's back and his right knee on the floor. "Take her to a room," he ordered Ali.

Ali grabbed Wilfrid's wife by the arm, and she wrestled with him. Ali slapped her on the cheek as she was about to scream for help.

"You scream, I'll kill you," Claude said as he pointed his gun toward her.

"Scream or not, you'll kill us anyway," Wilfrid's wife replied.

Claude shook his head, "No, you have nothing to do with this. It's between your husband and me. I promise I won't kill you if you stay quiet."

"Honey, do as he said, you'll be fine," Wilfrid advised his wife. She shook her head while tears rolled down her cheeks, and she walked toward her bedroom. Ali followed her.

"Please have mercy, please. I'm sorry for what I did. I was wrong, please forgive me. My wife is eight months pregnant. Please don't kill me," Wilfrid begged.

Claude shushed him before he put the muzzle of his Taurus Judge into Wilfrid's ass.

"I, I, I, I will do a, a, anything you want. That's my first child. Please don't kill me. God will bless you," the chief of the prison continued as he wept and trembled.

"You remember you said I will be pregnant by you. Well, I've brought you the baby," Claude said before he pulled the trigger twice. While incarcerated, Wilfrid had raped Claude a couple of times.

A few seconds later, the door of the bedroom opened, and Ali walked out. Claude stared at Ali who wiped his knife on the palm of his left hand. "What did you do to her?" Claude asked in confusion.

"I killed her," Ali replied.

"You what?" Claude snapped.

"You promised to keep her alive, but I didn't make any promise. She saw our faces, so she would have called the cops on us anyway. One less problem for us," Ali said with a mischievous smile.

For a second, Claude thought Ali was joking. He walked toward the bedroom to see what Ali had done. As soon as Claude opened the door, he covered his mouth with his hand at the sight of the woman dead on the floor. Ali had stabbed her a couple of times in the belly. Claude wiped his face with the palm of his hand and then scratched his head. He closed his eyes as he tried to understand what he'd just seen. He couldn't believe it. Claude stared at the woman on the floor for a couple of minutes with his mind racing, and then said, "Let's go."

Ali followed Claude, who exited the house. They both got on the bike and headed back to their slum. As they rode to the slum, Ali said a few things to Claude, but Claude remained quiet. Claude was disturbed by his henchman's act and felt his heart ache as though he were related to the victim. He wondered what kind of a man Ali was to have the courage to stab a pregnant woman multiple times in the belly. Claude regretted that he'd let Ali accompany him on this mission.

Claude hated collateral damage. He used the death of Anita, his mother, as an example. The members of the Iron Teeth had murdered his innocent mother when they came looking for his brother, Ronald. Anita had nothing to do with Ronald's involvement in illicit activities. Whenever Claude had to kill someone, he made sure he murdered only his target.

When they arrived back at Ali's home, Claude couldn't take it anymore. He decided to speak up. "For the sake of the child, you should have spared her life," Claude yelled as he slammed his Taurus Judge on the table and then kicked a chair.

"I ain't gonna lie to you. If she was here right now, I would have stabbed her again," Ali replied through gritted teeth.

Claude glared at Ali. He wanted to punch him in the face, but instead he grabbed his handgun and headed to the exit. He felt if he stayed any longer, things would get out of hand between him and Ali.

"We need to act as quickly as possible on that cop, and if you can't kill Leito, I'll take care of him. I won't make him suffer. I'll just cut his throat," Ali said.

Claude stopped walking and turned around.

"What are you doing?" Ali asked when he saw Claude pointing the gun at him.

"I thought my brother had the darkest heart, but I was wrong. You're pure evil."

"The friend of my enemy is my enemy. Leito must..." Before Ali even finished his sentence Claude pulled the trigger, and Ali fell on his knees. The bullet lodged in Ali's heart. With his eyes widened, Ali put his hand on his chest and then glared at Claude as blood dripped through his fingers.

"Leito forever will be my best friend," Claude added before he put another bullet into Ali's head. Claude had run out of patience. Since he liked Ali, he'd given him a chance to redeem himself, but Ali's thirst for killing Leito was beyond limit. Claude knew deep inside if Ronald had killed Leito, he would have killed Ronald, even though Ronald was his only brother.

Waiting to Die

I tried to stay busy as much as I could to avoid dealing with my agony. The quake had taken Miriam, my antidote, away from me. That Saturday morning, the fourth day following the disaster, I woke up feeling devastated. Miriam's death had caught up to me. A feeling of bitterness overwhelmed me and took away all my strength. Emotionally and physically, I was exhausted and depressed. I wanted no part of this life, and suicide seemed to be the only option I had left.

My brother, my sister, and Junior came up to me. They were concerned about my isolation. I looked disoriented.

"What's wrong, Leito?" my sister asked.

"I'm done with this life. I'm here waiting to die," I replied.

"Player, I don't have words to comfort you for your loss. We're no better than those who perished. But I believe if we're still alive, God has a plan for us," Junior said.

"Honestly, if death comes to me right now, it would be a relief. I would go without resisting for even a second," I replied.

"Remember you represent our father and mother. After God, you're all we have. Please don't give up on us," my brother said.

I glanced at each of them and could read in their eyes that they needed me. They had relied on me even before the earthquake. They spoke the truth. I sighed and then nodded. Both my brother and my sister extended their hands to me. I hesitated a bit before I took their hands, and they pulled me up. Junior patted my back twice to encourage me.

As I was sipping on some hot coffee, I realized if I had committed suicide and abandoned them in such a difficult time, the decision would have been selfish on my part. If I couldn't move forward for myself, at least I had to stay and fight for them. I had a moral obligation to continue leading them.

Later that afternoon around five-forty-five, Nahomi, Jean-Baptiste's cousin brought Leila and Hervé to me. Nahomi expressed her worries about Jean-Baptiste. She said Jean-Baptiste talked non-stop about death, life, and hell, and nothing he said made sense to her. Nahomi told me that she'd decided to stay with me instead. I told her that I believed Jean-Baptiste had become paranoid from lack of sleep and probably too much killing in the past few days— and on top of that the loss of his wife.

Leila always carried her asthma inhaler with her. For an unknown reason, this day she came to my house without it. When I asked Nahomi to go to her house and look for it, she told me she wouldn't go by herself, knowing Jean-Baptiste hadn't left the house yet. Leila then started wheezing. Junior wasn't there to go get the inhaler for her and it was getting dark. Against my desire, I went to Nahomi's house to retrieve the inhaler.

As I was about to enter the house, I heard a gunshot. At first, I thought Jean-Baptiste had killed himself, and my heart pounded. I stopped walking and wondered what I would say or do with his kids. I took a deep breath and started walking again. As soon as my feet reached the door, I heard Jean-Baptiste yowling in pain, and a male voice said, "You're good, but not that good for me." I recognized the voice of Claude. I pulled out a .25 Beretta Model 418 from my khaki pants and tiptoed into the house.

"I could have killed you before, but your kids were there. I didn't want them to see that. You killed my brother. I must avenge his death." Claude pointed his gun at Jean-Baptiste.

Pow, a shot fired, and Claude fell on the ground—dead. I'd put a bullet in the back of his head. I glared at Jean-Baptiste who held the right side of his chest with his left hand as blood dripped through his fingers. Claude had shot him. For a second I thought of putting a bullet into Jean-Baptiste's head as well.

Jean-Baptiste looked shocked when he saw me holding the gun. He realized that Adler was right when he said I had a gun. Jean-Baptiste could read the expression on my face that I wanted revenge. His eyes never left mine while wondering what my next move would be.

As much as I wanted him dead, I would never kill him because of Margaret and his kids. I put the gun back into my pocket and walked out. As I exited the house, I heard two more gunshots; Jean-Baptiste fired two additional bullets into Claude's head. I didn't care if Jean-Baptiste would live or die from the bullet wound. I mentioned nothing to Junior and Nahomi.

Follow Me

Two days later, around ten in the morning, I saw Junior running toward me.

"Leito, where's Jean-Baptiste?" Junior asked, out of breath.

"I don't know. What's going on?" I replied.

"I heard there are US soldiers at the airport right now. They've come for Americans who are in Haiti. We need to tell Jean-Baptiste so he can take his kids to the airport now. Since they're underage, their father will be able to go with them."

Margaret had a US visa and when she was pregnant she came to the US and gave birth to her children. She used to travel with them, but her husband was denied for an entry visa by the US embassy a few times. Both Leila and Hervé were American citizens.

"I'll go with you, but you'll talk to him," I said.

"What's wrong with you and Jean-Baptiste, lately?" Junior asked.

"I'll tell you one day."

Junior shook his head in disbelief and agreed to my terms. Once we arrived at Nahomi's house, we saw Jean-Baptiste, who was moaning in pain. Doctors had helped him with antibiotics and painkillers, but they couldn't remove the bullet from his chest. They lacked the equipment to do any major surgery.

Junior explained the opportunity to Jean-Baptiste, who agreed to it. We paid a guy to go underneath the rubble of Jean-Baptiste's house to look for the children's passports. Kinas drove us to the airport with Jean-Baptiste and his kids.

About twenty yards away, we spotted a huge crowd in front of the airport. Kinas stopped the car; he couldn't go any further. Jean-Baptiste, Junior, the kids, and I got out of the car and walked toward the entrance of the airport. People were fighting to enter the gates of the airport, and the US soldiers who were in charge of managing the crowd looked overwhelmed. Some people claimed they were

Americans, but failed to show any ID. They claimed they'd lost everything during the quake.

As we wondered how we would get Jean-Baptiste and his kids inside the airport, a man called out, "Jean-Baptiste, what are you doing here?"

"I'm trying to get my kids inside the airport," Jean-Baptiste replied.

I looked at the man's ID badge on his chest and noticed that he was a cop. Maisonneuve Pradel was his name.

"Do you have their passports with you?" Maisonneuve asked.

"Yes I do."

"Good, follow me," Maisonneuve said to Jean-Baptiste.

I kissed Hervé and Leila on their cheeks and wished them luck. I felt relieved at the thought of their not having to deal with the aftermath of the disaster. I gave Jean-Baptiste a handshake, and he held my hands.

"I have a question for you," he said.

"Go ahead," I replied.

"Have you ever killed a man before Claude?" Jean-Baptiste asked.

"I always believed you were one of the best friends I ever had, but I was wrong. You're so self-centered. I helped your family and saved your life, not even a thank you. Miriam died and you never said anything. Did you know she died while she was also pregnant with my child?" I replied as I pulled my hand away from his.

"I, I, I..." Jean-Baptiste stammered.

"Yeah, I, I, I. what? You don't give a shit about anyone else. All you think about is you."

Jean-Baptiste stared at me and tried to figure out what words he should say to correct his mistakes. I removed myself from his presence and headed toward the car. At that moment, Junior understood the reason behind the tension between Jean-Baptiste and me.

When Junior got into the car, he handed me a photo. In that photo, Claude and I had our arms wrapped around each other's neck, and we were smiling at each other, while Ronald held a trophy in his hands. We looked so innocent and happy in that picture—we had won a soccer tournament. That photo brought back many memories. I reminisced about those days when my mother thought I was in church, while I was in the streets with Ronald and Claude riding bikes, or dancing at Rara, a music festival in Haiti during Easter. Ronald taught me how to ride a motorcycle and street fight. It also saddened me to know that I'd killed my childhood best friend.

Go Home Kid

Jean-Baptiste and his children going to the US meant one less worry for me. He called me a couple of times to inform me about the adaptation of his kids and his recovery. Jean-Baptiste told me his chest wound had been infected by the time he underwent the surgery to remove the casing inside of him. Whenever I spoke to Leila and Hervé, they sounded happy. If I had the power, I would have sent away all children under twelve years of age who were in the cities devastated by the quake.

Port-au-Prince and the other cities affected by the disaster looked more like charnel houses than anything else. We had to cut the branches off the trees and burn the leaves to chase away the stench of the dead. Debris, rubble, tents, and dust everywhere added to the problem of lack of portable water.

As much as I was grateful for the international aid and all the efforts made around the world to help Haiti get back on its feet following the disaster, my heart ached at the sight of the distribution of the humanitarian aid. Jean Jacques Dessalines, Toussaint Louverture, Henri Christophe, and many other great ancestors would have never pictured their sons and daughters begging for food and depending on the international aid after every single disaster. Haiti, the richest colony in the seventeenth century labeled as the poorest country in the Western Hemisphere two centuries later. Within weeks, Haiti became the republic of non-governmental organizations and the country of tents.

Every day, I stopped by Mona's and spent at least an hour on top of the rubble where Miriam had perished. As soon I as sat down on top of the debris, I said, "Good afternoon, Ms. Commando, my angel." In a monologue, I would tell her about my day and how much I missed her and our child. I reminisced about all the sweet memories with Miriam. I found myself smiling at the thought of Miriam's jokes, her love, and her care toward me. I would save the tears for later when I got home. I would never get over Miriam's early departure for eternity. Before I went home, I would say, "I love you, angel, please kiss our child for me."

I didn't know if the country had mental health providers at this time. If it did I wouldn't have been able to afford it. That *one hour* a day was my therapy and gave me strength day by day to embrace the many obstacles in my path and move on with my life. I had been heartbroken before, but when the earthquake killed Miriam, it stole my heart.

The second week of February 2010, I went back to work. When I got paid, I gave money to Mona to help her attend to her needs.

"You don't have to do all this," Mona said to me one day.

"That's the least I can do. If I were the one who'd died, Miriam would have done the same for my family, and even more," I replied.

Mona nodded and acknowledged the truth of my statement. She knew her daughter was a loving and caring person. Miriam helped many people during her short life, and Judith was living proof of Miriam's generosity.

"I thought you would have hated me for not only refusing you for my daughter, but also causing her death and the death of the child of yours she carried," Mona confessed.

"I forgave you because you were only protecting your daughter," I replied. I had no reason to hate Mona. Even if I did, hating Mona wouldn't bring Miriam back to life. I had enough on my plate, and hatred would just make my heart heavier or kill my soul more quickly. I forgave myself for killing my childhood best friend. I forgave Jean-Baptiste and Mona.

"What's killing me the most is the fact that since the day of the quake Raul stopped by once, and he never visited me again. I wished I could have seen in you what Miriam saw that made her want you so much. That's my biggest mistake and regret of my entire life. I don't know if I can live with that," Mona said in sorrow.

"I was lost, and Miriam rescued me. She showed me the way to love again. Miriam was everything I ever wanted and dreamt of in love," I admitted in turn.

"I believe that a child of yours and Miriam's would have been one of the most beautiful children on earth," Mona stated.

"I imagine the same thing every single day."

"I always prayed to the Lord to grant me the blessing of seeing my grandchildren before I died. He granted me the wish, and I destroyed it," Mona said as tears rolled down her cheeks. She started crying.

I wrapped my right arm around her neck to comfort her. "The Lord has given, the Lord has taken. Glory be the name of the Lord," I replied as I looked up to the sky to prevent tears from falling down my cheeks. The pain was beyond my strength. I sobbed and wiped my face with the palm of my hand.

After that conversation, Mona joined me at the top of the rubble every day. She would tell me stories of her past, the way she met and married Enock, Miriam's father, and many other stories. Some of her stories made me laugh. I wanted to share with her a few things of my life as well, but the respect I had for her prevented me from doing so. She vented, and I listened. Mona described the life of her daughter to me step by step, from the day Miriam was born to the day she died on January 12, 2010. I believe that was her therapy.

"Go home, kid. It's getting dark. I'll see you tomorrow," Mona would say to me.

I would obey her and go home with the hope that God would allow me to see her the next day. I could see Mona was hurt and dying inside. I represented some kind of life support for her.

Again

On the second Sunday of July 2010, I went to church and asked God for a better job or for an opportunity to study abroad. I prayed with faith and I believed it was a matter of time before I witnessed a miracle in my life. I sent my resume to different companies and organizations.

On August 31, 2010, Save the Children offered me twelve-hundred US dollars per month as an auditor. On September 1, 2010, Catholic Relief Services, an international non-governmental organization offered me an auditing position for fourteen-hundred US dollars per month, including transportation. That same afternoon, I had an appointment to pick up my passport with a student visa to go to the US. The Metropolitan College of New York (MCNY) had selected me as one of six Haitian students to earn a master's degree in Emergency and Disaster Management.

God had answered my prayers. I thanked God for all my undeserved blessings. As I sat on my bed to contemplate all the miracles God had bestowed upon me, I replayed in my mind and my heart the following lyrics of a song, "Even the angels in heaven can't understand God's love for me." When I reviewed my spiritual life, I realized I did so many things wrong, and yet God never stopped loving me.

I found myself unable to sleep, having such a dilemma—go for the master's or stay and work. Many people I sought advice from told me to take the job. I called Jean-Baptiste to get his opinion. He said, "Now they say that's what they want to give you, but when you come back with that degree you'll tell them how much you want to be paid."

The next morning, I booked my ticket. I had a dream to live. Money would come one day. I packed my clothes and then went to see some of my family and friends to tell them about my departure for New York City.

September 3, 2010 was a very special day in my life. Not only was my dream of earning a master's degree in the US coming true, but also instead of picking up or dropping people off at the airport, it was my time to be on the other side of the gate and catch my plane. I hugged my brother and kissed my sister on the forehead. I told them I loved them and advised them to remain strong and behave themselves.

"Be patient, your day will soon come," I said to Junior before I hugged him.

I looked at them, seeing their eyes filled with tears of joy. I felt heartbreak as I waved goodbye to them.

As soon as the plane took off and was in the air, a Caucasian lady who appeared to be in her fifties, pulled out her phone from her bag and played, "Ain't No Sunshine" by Bill Withers. As soon as the music started playing, tears flooded my cheeks, and I leaned my head against the window.

"Did you lose your family during the earthquake?" the woman asked me.

"Yes, my girlfriend… She was pregnant with my child."

The woman didn't add a single word. She pulled me against her, and I rested my head on her lap. She rubbed my head to comfort me as though I were her child. I reminisced about the days I'd spent with Miriam. I told the woman to play the song one more time because it helped me cry out all my pain, my loss, and suffering. That day I didn't hold back. A few minutes later, a deep slumber came to my rescue.

Later on, the Caucasian woman told me she'd lost her entire family during the disaster: her husband and two kids. They were tourists in Haiti. Just before the quake, she couldn't get a good signal to place a call. She stepped out of the hotel and a few seconds later, she found herself covered with dust. The beautiful hotel they'd stayed at crumbled to the ground and left behind no survivors.

I was mesmerized by the beauty of the landscape as the plane got closer to land. Like in Haiti, I thought JFK Airport had one terminal, so I didn't mention what airline I was flying with. I ended up spending about five hours at JFK before being picked up. *Welcome to New York, Leito.*

I had to go to MCNY to complete my paperwork. As I stood on the corner of Canal and Varrick Street waiting for the green light, the ground shook beneath my feet. I panicked and said, "Again." I became paranoid and thought the earthquake had followed me all the way to New York City. When I looked around and saw everyone remaining calm, I realized the vibration was the subway moving beneath the street.

The Metropolitan College of New York and New York City Council member Mathieu Eugene organized a welcome ceremony in Borough Hall for us—the six Haitian students. People greeted us with enthusiasm and were eager to hear words from each of us. That night, I felt like a star in Hollywood. Journalist flooded us with photos and pulled me here and there to get an interview.

As I smiled to take pictures, I thought about the days I sacrificed pleasure for education. Instead of buying clothes and shoes, I used the money sent by my uncle and my adoptive mother to pay my school tuition. I looked up and said, "Thank you, Momma, I hope you're happy and proud of me. I wish you were here to share this moment with me." When I reached home, I watched the news and I heard that a tornado had hit not far from where they'd held the ceremony. After hurricanes and an earthquake, I was then introduced to tornadoes.

I had a stressful and difficult first semester at MCNY. I could barely understand what my teachers and classmates were saying. The way they pronounced the words was different from the way I did. On top of that, certain people made language matters difficult for me. Anytime I talked they said, "You have an accent." So I tried to talk as little as possible until one of my professors came to me and said, "Don't be afraid to speak, because when you do, you draw attention to yourself."

I didn't believe her at first until I focused more on my environment and realized she was right. I threw away my fear of speaking and improved my accent by listening and speaking more. Everyone has an accent; it all depends on your location and your origin.

I was introduced to a new educational system. Instead of my professors writing all the notes on the board, I had to write and read a lot. I turned the library into my new home—books in one hand, dictionary in the other hand, and Google in front of me. I felt if I failed, it would affect my reputation as a man and the reputation of the country I represented. At the end of the semester, I passed all my classes.

I used to watch snow on TV. Seeing it falling from the sky and being able to hold it in my hands brought joy to my soul. I never thought snow, a beautiful, white, refined powder from the sky could paralyze an entire city. For New Yorkers, the blizzard of Christmas 2010 was a disaster, to me—a fun experience.

Get Down

I had a very good time at the Metropolitan College of New York. I graduated with a master's in Public Administration in June 2012. I did an internship at the Salvation Army with some great guys, Craig, Ian, and Rico who worked in the disaster services. They took me to a couple of places in New Jersey and upstate New York. I went to Nassau County to help out during Hurricane Irene.

The night after my graduation ceremony, I went to an all-white party in Queens with my friend Mikelson. We had a blast. Mikelson and I used to play for our local soccer team before he moved to New York in 2005. Since I wanted to explore a bit the nightlife of NYC, one of my classmates advised me to go to a lounge called The Flow on West 3rd Street. He said I would find many college girls and international students as well.

On Friday night, July 6, 2012, I took the B train and headed to The Flow. Once I got in front of the lounge, I looked in the glass windows and saw a young crowd having fun. I couldn't wait to get in. The bouncer in front of the lounge asked me for my ID, and I handed it to him. Before the bouncer even got a chance to give it back to me, he grabbed the collar of my shirt and said, "Get down." He jumped over another person in line and ducked with her behind a car. It was total chaos. Two guys in a Cadillac were firing at people in front of the lounge.

While on the ground, I covered my head with my hands as though they were bulletproof and could save me. At first, I thought someone had sent those shooters to kill me. My heart pounded so hard that I thought I'd have a heart attack. I hadn't felt fear like that since the earthquake, and this was much worse.

The incident happened so fast that I couldn't recall much of it afterward. When I stood up, I saw bullet holes in the glass doors exactly where I had been standing. That bouncer was an angel and a hero—he saved my life and the woman's life. I glanced around me and I saw a man dead on the sidewalk with his brain matter all over the place and the woman holding the bouncer in her hands and crying hysterically for help—the bouncer had been shot. I heard somebody call out to the woman, "Laurie." The police and ambulance arrived on the scene quickly. They stabilized the bouncer and took him to the nearest hospital.

I jumped into a yellow cab and went back home to Brooklyn.

"Fifty-two dollars, sir" the taxi driver said when I stopped in front of the apartment where I lived.

"Fifty-two?" I mumbled, and I took three twenty-dollar bills out of my wallet and paid the driver. As I opened the door, I became pissed. The ride cost me that much when I could simply have taken the B train and paid two dollars and fifty cents. I learned my lesson the hard way. I filled a cup with warm water from the sink and went to my room.

I heard on the news that the bouncer who'd saved me made it alive to the hospital. I wished my country had such good infrastructure to save more lives. I would do anything in my power to meet this man and thank him one day. I soon after heard the bouncer became famous following the sale of his book called *Guilty of Natural Beauty,* and was soon to be married to a woman named Barbara.

If I Had Stayed

The second week of August 2012, Junior phoned me.

"Yo, yo, what's up, player?" he said.

"Chilling, player," I replied.

"I don't have many minutes on my phone. I have good news and bad news for you."

"Tell me the good part first," I said.

"My aunt helped me with some cash, and I'm going to Chile next week," Junior said.

"That's great. player. I told you your time would come soon. What's the bad news?"

"Mona passed away," Junior said.

"What? Was she sick?" I yelled.

"I don't think so, player. She couldn't live with the guilt of knowing Miriam died because of her. I believe sorrow killed her."

"An entire family disappeared in smoke."

"*C'est la vie.*"

As I sat on my bed thinking about life, my guilt haunted me again. *If only I had stayed.* The night before my mother died, she'd asked me to stay with her. I told her no, and I went to my grandmother's house, one of the decisions I regretted and couldn't forgive myself for. I had heard different stories about my mother's passing. The closest neighbors believed that my father had something to do with my mother's death. I couldn't deny such a fact because instead of looking for help within the neighborhood, my father walked about a half-mile to go to my grandmother's house to seek help. The neighbors said that my father locked the door, and no one could get into the house.

My father disliked me because I discovered the secret voodoo paraphernalia he hid within the house. He would hide mystical bottles underneath the bed, within the walls, and anywhere it would have been impossible for other people to see them—but I always spotted them and told my mom right away. He hated me for that. Everyone said I looked just like my father. However, we never got along. I was born with a special skill that helped me detect anything supernatural.

My father was singing in the men's choir at his church and still going to visit voodoo priests in secret. Even though my father had all those flaws, he was still my father, and I loved him very much. When I put all the facts together, though, I found forgiving him for my mother's death difficult.

My father had a crazy ambition to become rich overnight. He was also seeing other women. He didn't find my mother beautiful any longer. Yet my father seemed to forget that my mother was the one taking care of the household expenses since he had been fired from a beverage company affiliated with Coca-Cola. In his head, once he got rid of my mom, he would live happily forever after with another more beautiful woman.

Two days after my mom died, he came up to me and tried to comfort me with those words, "Don't cry. I know we've lost your mom, but we'll become rich. I'll take good care of you."

Even though I was devastated by the loss of my mother, his speech gave me some comfort. The man who never liked me told me that he would take good care of me. I saw a new beginning with better finances. Well the joke was on me. Within a few months, he spent all our resources by going to different cities within our country to visit the famous voodoo priests. He claimed he was seeking revenge because my mother didn't die from natural causes. He went places where his best friend, Harold, advised him to go.

Harold was a neighbor who lived a few yards away from my parents' house. He was my father's best friend. My mother considered him a brother and loved him very much. My mother was his maid of honor. Harold played the role of an advisor for my parents. They made him aware of anything they had in mind, from buying another piece of land to expanding the business, Harold knew all about my family. Like my father, Harold had lost his job. He then became jealous of the financial progress of my parents.

A few days after my mother's funeral, Harold came up to me and asked me about the dress my mother had on during her time at the morgue. I told him I had no clue about it. My father had given me a well-tied black plastic bag with some clothes in it—my mother's clothes. He told me never to mention this to anyone and to take the secret to the grave.

When someone was killed by supernatural means, the killer could sell the soul of the victim for power or wealth in return. That soul would be doomed to work as a slave till the end of time. The clothes the deceased had on during his or her time in the morgue represented the key.

Ten months after my mother's death, my father passed away. He came up to me one day, pulled out a rock from his pocket, and told me that someone had hit him with that rock in the middle of his head. When I touched his parietal lobe, I couldn't believe it. The part hit by the rock was no longer a bone, but like a muscle. I pushed my fingers through it, and I felt as if I'd touched his brain.

My father claimed the attack was from the supernatural world, so he went to his mother's house in the countryside. Within a few days following his arrival, my father died, and none of his children attended his funeral. In fact, my brother, my sister, and I only became aware of our father's death a few weeks later. They reported to me that before my father died, he became mentally ill and started talking to himself. The day he died, blood came out of his nose, his eyes, his mouth, and all the other orifices in his body.

Some people said that my grandmother, my mother's mother, used dark magic to kill my father to avenge her daughter. Others stated that my father went to a couple of voodoo temples where he had the voodoo priests work on his behalf, and then he never paid them for their services. Therefore, they took his life.

Although I never received a good explanation for my parents' deaths, the passing of my mother mystified me the most. The different stories about my mom's death tormented me. Whenever I saw my mom in my dreams, she looked happy. One night in my dream, I asked her, "Who killed you?"

"Turn around and look who's coming," she said.

I was shocked to see my father coming toward me in that dream. When I asked my father the same question, he pointed out Harold, who was walking behind him. As real as the dream seemed to be, I couldn't believe it. In their journey toward becoming rich, my father and Harold plotted against my mother. Since Harold couldn't get the dress, he killed my father. That dream troubled my heart and soul. I would never have expected something like that from Harold or my father.

After that dream, I went to Harold's house and asked him to give me back my mother's rings. I knew he had the rings. I wondered how and when he took them, but I never asked him that question. Harold had given both of my mother's rings to his wife. He told me that he'd kept them as a memory of my mother. Harold gave me back only the wedding ring. He stated that his wife had lost her engagement ring, so he kept my mother's.

Every time I slept with the ring on my finger, I would have nightmares and find myself fighting with all kind of demons. Emotionally, the ring represented a burden for me, but I carried it anyway since I was the first born in my family. One day as I was playing with the ring, it fell off in front of me in muddy water, I looked for it, but it was gone.

Another time, Harold gave me a can of chocolate powder. I struggled to remove the plastic cap. I found that odd. When I took a closer look at the can, I spotted that it had been opened before and resealed with glue. I walked outside and threw it in the sewer.

Three days later, Harold asked me, "Did you drink the chocolate?"

"Yes, I did." I lied because I didn't want to hurt his feelings.

Less than a week later, Harold asked me the same question. I looked him straight in the eyes and said, "Yes I did, and anytime you have more, give it to me."

My answer and stare told him everything. Harold understood that I knew something. From that day on, our relationship was changed. Whenever Harold saw me, he hid or took another route. After that day, he never offered me anything else. Harold used to come visit me at my grandmother's house, but he stopped all of that.

If I had stayed when she asked me, maybe my mother would be still alive. I missed her so much; she was the only person in the entire world who understood my personality and loved me regardless. I would have been a physician instead of being an accountant. I always wanted to be a pediatrician, but when my mother passed away, I chose a field of study that could bring me money more quickly.

If I had stayed, maybe Claude wouldn't have become an assassin. Many innocent lives could have been spared, including Marc's, Richard and his family, and many others. I wouldn't have murdered my childhood best friend.

If I had stayed, my mom would have been able to provide me with money. I would have been able to take care of Miriam and save her. I would have been able to witness the growing up of my child with Miriam. I would have married Miriam and made her one of the happiest women in the world. I would have worked and built a home in Jacmel to live with her and our children. I wanted to have three children with her. I would have taken her to Paris and made love to her in a way we never did. With all the *Ifs*, I could probably go back in time to when earth was a paradise and told Eve not to eat the forbidden fruit.

The End

About The Author

Born and raised in Haiti, Elie Jerome started writing poetry when he was 13 years old after the death of his mother. Writing became his escaped route. Elie is a graduate of Metropolitan College of New York and also the author of the love triangle romance, *I Dare You To Try It*.

His goal is to allow his readers to connect and even to believe they will meet one day the characters he creates. With a unique and easy read style, he gives the readers vivid stories that are breathtaking, fascinating, full of twists, and mind-blowing. Read him once and become his fan forever.

Contact info:

eliejerome8@gmail.com

www.eliejerome1.com